A NOTE FROM THE AUTHOR

This edition of Guardians of Felina: Rise of the Phantom represents a complete reimagining of the original release. With expanded world-building, deepened character arcs, additional new internal artwork, and updated chapter pacing, this version better reflects the story I always wanted to tell.

If you've read the earlier edition, welcome back – and thank you. If this is your first time in the world of Felina, I hope you love what's ahead.

~Elora Sofa

For information regarding permission and other media inquiries, visit:

www.elorasofia.com

ISBN 978-1-7354958-6-6

29 28 27 26 25 24 23   23 24 25 26 27 28

Printed in the U.S.A.

First printing November 2024. Now retired. Second edition printing August 2025.

GUARDIANS OF FELINA

Rise of the Phantom

Second Edition

ELORA SOFIA

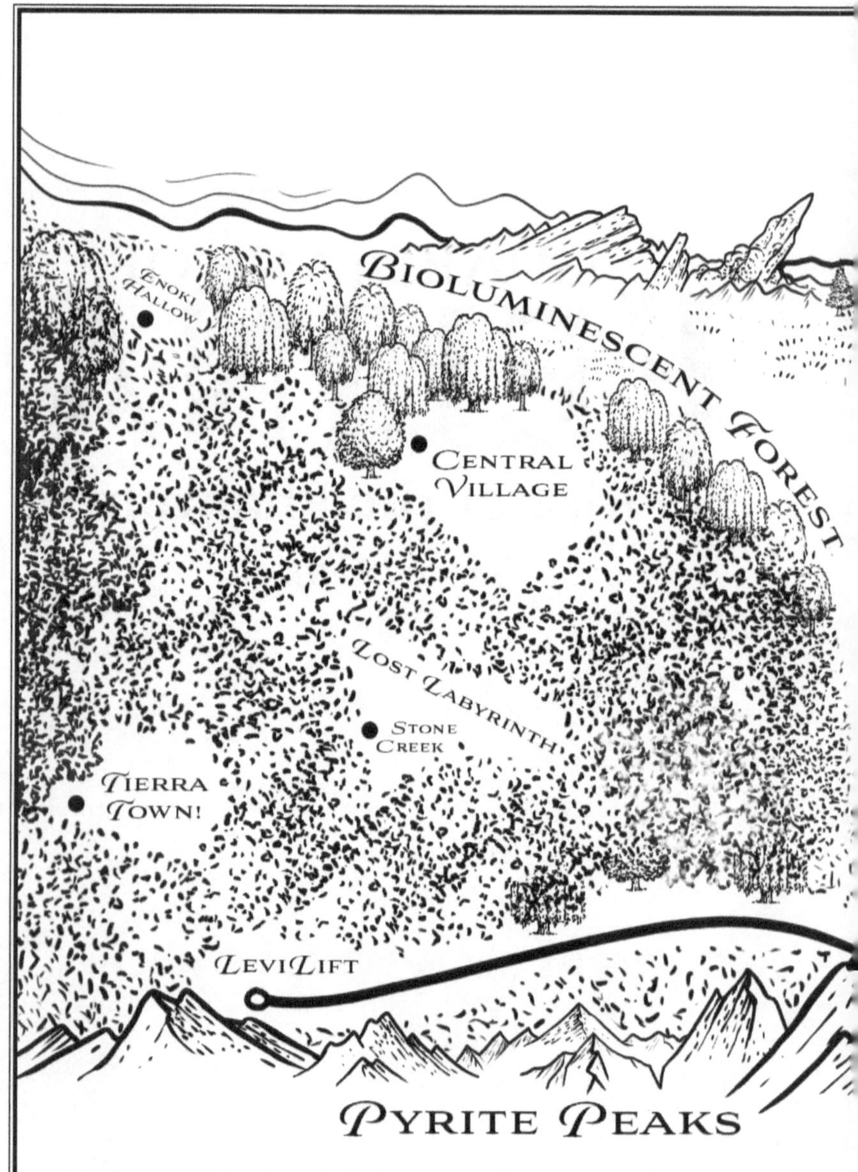

Bioluminescent Forest
Enoki Hallow
Central Village
Lost Labyrinth
Stone Creek
Tierra Town!
LeviLift
Pyrite Peaks

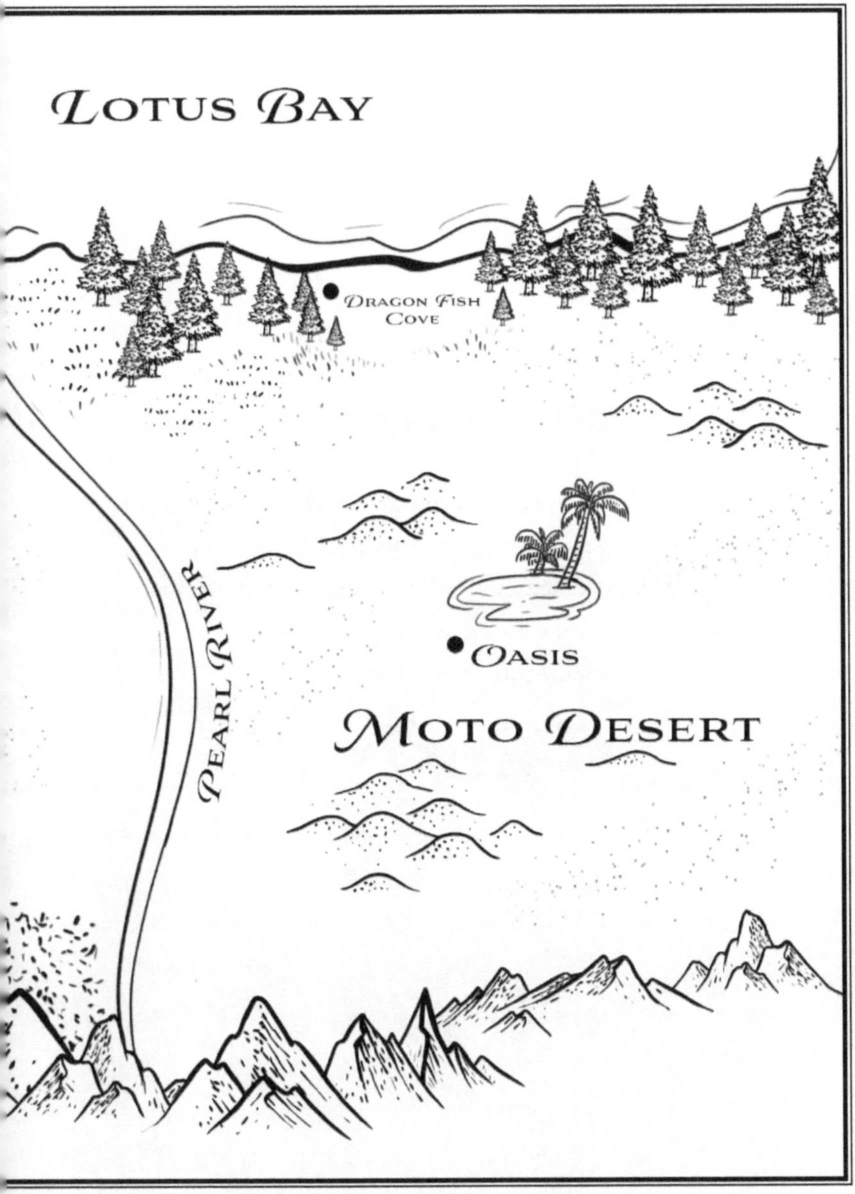

Lotus Bay
Dragon Fish Cove
Pearl River
Oasis
Moto Desert

Dedicated to Melanie, the best mommy. Thank you for making my story happen. Thank you for being there every step of the way: extensive brainstorming, helping with my writer's block, editing, and your endless support and love!

Pronunciation

Alada: Ah-LAH-dah
Tierra: Tee-EHR-ah
Coralees: Core-AHL-lees
Ember: EHM-bur
Birch: Bur-ch
Gnarla: NAR-lah
Ara: AR-rah (Plural: Aras – AR-rah-s)
Nya: NEE-yah (Plural: Nyas – NEE-yah-s)
Mizu: MEE-zoo (Plural: Mizus – MEE-zoo-s)
Meu: Me-ew (Plural: Meus – Me-ew-s)
Umbrakin: Um-bruh-kin

Table of Contents

The Prophecy

Long ago, some several thousand years, a prophecy came into existence from a well-known seer. By the order of Source, the creator of all, four parts of the prophecy were to be given to each territory to encourage a greater community.

Leaders came together, putting their piece to the puzzle onto the table for others to read. After reading the whole prophecy, the leaders agreed to burn their individual pieces after transcribing all four onto one parchment. In the name of unity and peace, the prophecy was going to be made available for all to see.

Later that night, one lone cat crept into where the parchment lay – beyond the sleeping guards. As he reached out and picked it up, the guardsman's staff clanged down upon the ground – waking him to a sight of this male cat holding the prophecy above the flames within the grand fireplace.

Before the guard could reach him, the cat began to burn the parchment. Though the guard tackled him to the floor, the parchment continued to burn and was only snuffed out once out of the grip of the angered traitor. Now, only one part of the prophecy remained, but the other three parts – were gone.

As decided, the leaders still put forth the prophecy, what remained of it, to all. The message spread across the world in this land of ancient times, but somehow, not even the leaders of the other three parts could remember what was on it. Their inability to remember caused chaos as some thought it could be an opportunity to insert themselves as a Guardian, create new insertions, or dictate the rules of how Guardianship would be chosen. But nothing could change the truth of Source's words, regardless of whether they remembered the correct words or not.

From the nameless Seer of the Bioluminescent Forest:

Set forth by the Source of all
Let it be known to all the world
Of the Creation of Guardianship

Four great Guardians shall emerge
Unknown be the time or day
Chosen of courage, strength, and care
To protect and support all beings

But behold, a day shall dawn when —

With the prophecy burned and lost to time, egos eventually gave way to a Great War, spurred on by desires for conquest and control—fueled, in part, by an invading species whose identity was wiped from history and left only as a vague myth whispered through the ages.

As if the war would never end, the first Guardian was chosen—not only to bring the conflict to a close but to act as a liaison between the Source, the Great Spirit and creator of all, and the Guardians yet to come. The Guardians were created to ensure longevity and prosperity across the land. Chosen for her distinctly pure and deeply maternal nature, a gentle, kindly, and quiet Nya named Alada was brought into the Guardianship, though she rarely speaks of how this came to be, or what the transformation entailed.

Her first decree, which she set for herself, was to end the Great War. Her second was to return the world of Felina to a trade-based economy, hoping to build long-term peace and foster a spirit of cooperation across the realms.

For several centuries, Alada protected all of Felina as the sole Guardian. She reestablished trade routes and allowed each territory to pursue its own path—spiritually, emotionally, physically, and technologically. As the cherished Guardian of the Pyrite Peaks, she welcomed anyone from any region who sought her wisdom and guidance.

She watched as the Nyas, over generations, channeled their collective strength into hollowing out the mountain while sharpening their sword-fighting skills to levels unmatched anywhere else in Felina. Whispers among inventors revealed dreams of building a fortress like no other, filled with ingenious conveniences.

In the Bioluminescent Forest, the Meus deepened their communion with Spirit, aligning their homes and lives with the divine rhythms of nature.

The Aras of the Moto Desert, ever loyal to tradition, continued steadily on the ancient path laid by their ancestors—unchanging, unwavering, guided by ceremony and custom.

The Mizus—cats of the water—captured Alada's curiosity most of all. They began experimenting with compacting sand into a concrete-like material to build homes and eventually raised a town along the shoreline. Their success defied conventional knowledge, yet they shared little of how it worked.

Being winged and of the air, Alada could not follow them into the depths. The Mizus, with their miraculous tails and gills, lived much of their lives beneath the sea. Still, every so often, they surfaced with inventions that stunned even her. Technologically, they were advancing faster than the other regions, though how remained a mystery.

Alada watched over them all as her own children—until the day she no longer stood alone.

Over the next century, three more Guardians emerged. Alada continued to watch over the lands, guiding each Guardian in turn, until only her own territory remained in her direct care.

In time, with each Guardian fully established, Alada encouraged them to step back from their populations—intervening only in dire emergencies. She believed each realm should be free to grow and evolve on its own terms, uninfluenced by divine hands. As their leader, she led by example, retreating from the public eye and becoming a figure of folklore, passed down in kitten tales and bedtime whispers.

One by one, the others followed her path into legend. But not completely.

Chapter 1

The Bioluminescent Forest

The grains of sand spun into a glowing circle, like a serpent made of glass. A portal.

"Are you ready?" the hooded figure asked.

The icy-calm voice sent shivers down his spine. "Always am. Where to?" the sandy, charcoal-black cat replied with a flick of his tail.

"The largest forest around," the hooded figure answered.

As wind swept over the dunes, the figure twirled its fingers gently. The sparkling circle expanded, its serpent-like spiral widening into a shimmering window. Beyond it, a glowing forest shimmered through the light.

Anger has brought me this far already. No turning back now.

Without hesitation, the black cat stepped through, the hooded figure close behind.

✧ ✧ ✧

She waited.

Perched at the cliff's edge, her white wings folded neatly

at her sides, she watched the moment the sun crested the horizon. And when it did… she leapt.

Gliding over and around the territories with her wings outstretched brought such peace. Watching her waking cats in the mornings, the Nyas of the Pyrite Peaks, helped her not feel so lonely. She and the other three Guardians had vowed to remain hidden from the cats of each region—except for young kittens—so the world wouldn't grow dependent on them. But still… she knew this wouldn't last forever.

When the mountains and tall pines cleared away, she instinctively gained altitude. After a while, her stomach rumbled with a growl. *The irony of immortality,* she thought. The question was *what* to eat today? Mouse? Rabbit…? Chicken…? FEESH! Yes, that's what — feesh. With three playful flips, she soared toward Lotus Bay. Her gray eyes sparkled blue as the Purcific Ocean spread out beneath her, a smile dawning on her face as she glided over a Mizu village nestled among clusters of salt-sap trees.

She dove into the shimmering blue sea, catching both a surface-dwelling rat-fish and a clam-eyed tuna. Flying to the shore, she landed on a barnacle-covered rock to eat, but as she opened her mouth, a small voice startled her.

"Mizz, can we eat some of your feesh pweeze? We hungwee."

She thought she had chosen an uncharted beach to catch her fish, but as she turned to see who had spoken to her, it was not just one but three tiny Mizus. They were tiny and sopping wet, literally dripping. *They must have been trying to hunt in the water.* She felt a swelling in her chest and could not resist. "Certainly," she mewed as she handed them her tuna. "Good thing I caught two."

She always loved Mizu kittens with their large apricot eyes, sleek ocean-blue fur, and tails with large fins on the end to help with speed in the water. Mizus always reminded her of Coralees, Guardian and goddess of Lotus Bay, who had similar features.

The three kittens tore at the flesh speedily, as if they had not had food for a thousand years.

"Watch for bones," she whispered.

When they swallowed the last bit of meat, the first kitten meowed, "Fwank you, Mizz…?"

"Isn't it obveeis? It's Corwalweez!" mewed the second.

"No, it's *SorwalBEES!*" the third rudely corrected, poking the other in the shoulder.

"Why are we asking her name and not telwing her ours? I'm Bubble, this is Dewdrop, and she is Puddle," said Bubble.

Alada choked back a giggle as she told them, "I'm Alada Gata, Guardian and goddess of the Pyrite Peaks. I'm not *Coralees*, but I do know her."

The three of them gasped in awe.

"Wow!" Puddle meowed. "You wook like her."

"But prettier," Dewdrop purred.

"And wid wings," Bubble added.

Puddle scrunched her forehead, deep in thought. "Actually, you don't look like her at all."

"Told ya," Dewdrop said.

"No, you didn't!"

Alada's heart dropped a notch when audible pawsteps in the salt-sap forest grew in the distance. *I have to go,* she thought with an ache in her heart. Watching the kittens stuff fish in their faces brought a smile to her lips, yet she gave them her other fish, said farewell, and flew off around a bend. She circled back though, landing on top of a tall salt-sap tree known for its, well … salty sap. She licked her fingers, fantasizing about the fish she had caught and given away, smothered in salt-sap. The tree was a good quarter mile away — enough to ensure that the other cat running toward the kittens was out for the young Mizu's safety.

"Honeys, I told you not to stay out long without one of us!" a female voice called.

"We were on our way home, but we got hungwy," Bubble stated.

"And we could not catch *anyfing*. It was all just too fast!" Dewdrop complained.

"But *den* we met Awada Gata, and she gave us her feesh!" Puddle finished.

"That's nice. Now, it's time you three had a bath and dinner," the female said, ushering the kittens back toward the local village.

The pawsteps faded, leaving only the crash of distant waves. She exhaled slowly, watching them roll in and out.

Joy was fleeting. Company was borrowed. And when laughter faded, the ache of solitude returned. She needed someone who understood her — more than the occasional kitten. Before she unraveled. She needed to reset her mind — to swap sadness for silliness. If anyone could do that, it was Tierra.

Well, maybe Coral? She was already in her territory after all. *Less flying,* she thought. *The only problem is the whole not being able to breathe underwater thing.* Ember's territory was the next closest, but empathy and companionship weren't in Ember's vocabulary, so to speak.

So, Tierra it was. *The Bioluminescent Forest,* she sighed. She'd already done more flying than expected today. *Maybe she'll have some food to spare?* She leaped out of the tree and glided on the south wind current toward the Bioluminescent Forest.

The sun was positioned precisely overhead by the time Alada selected a spot to land and begin her search on paw. She stood before a heavily wooded thicket — or at least the closest thing to an edge this forest seemed to have. Still, there was no mistaking it. "I remember Tierra spending a lot of time near Central Village. I'll head that way."

But first, she needed to get her bearings. The dense moss-bushes tangled around her feet, and mourning vines draped from the upper branches of towering cedar trees. The shift from sunlight to bioluminescence was always a bit disorienting.

"I'll head that way... once I'm oriented, anyway," she muttered, scanning the dimming forest floor. "Central Village… maybe a bit more south."

Her eyes caught on a tiger tooth lily — its petals curled with striking orange and black stripes, and a ring of sharp white in the center gave it a toothy appearance. "Poisonous and native to the Central Village region," she recited. "Antidote is lion's mane, always found within five feet. Symbiotic growth."

Sure enough, the shaggy mushroom clung to the bark of a nearby moss-bush.

Alada glanced out over the glowing horizon and sighed. *Why haven't we come up with a better way to find each other?* she wondered. *How am I supposed to locate one Guardian in an entire forest?*

She trekked onward, weaving through gnarled trunks and dense undergrowth. "It's been a while," she murmured. "Trees… there sure are a lot of them."

Despite the forest canopy barely allowing any sunlight to reach the floor, it was surprisingly bright, not dark. Glowing flowers and mushrooms of blue and green gave off a gentle aura, illuminating her path. The springy peat underneath her paws felt almost bouncy and the whole place smelled of leaf-mold, flowers, moss, and fresh water.

I know Tierra likes it here because of the trees, but it's rather cramped for me. Breathe and focus on the beauty. She folded her feathered white wings close to her body.

Alada hadn't been among the Meus—the feline inhabitants of the Bioluminescent Forest—for what felt like a very long time because it *had* been a very long time. So long, in fact, that her memories of them felt more like dreams than memories.

She thought back to the ancient war, when the peaceful Meus stunned the mighty warriors of her own realm, the Nyas, with a ferocity no one expected. *They certainly do fight to defend themselves,* she mused, stepping over a crawling vine.

Tierra often spoke of the Meus: their swirling fur patterns, long fluffy tails, and their deep bond with the forest itself. She never failed to boast about her own lovely pale-orange and amber tabby coat, or her unmatched skills in hide-and-seek.

Vanity might be Tierra's only weakness, Alada thought—but she was still a fierce Guardian who loved her cats deeply.

As Alada continued through the humid undergrowth, she worked to keep her claustrophobia in check. The glowing canopy above pressed inward, but she focused on the delightful shimmer and scent of moss and flowers.

Just as she was about to step down, glowing mushroom rings materialized beneath her paw. She paused. *Tierra did say that kind of thing is normal around here...* She stepped over them while lifting the low hanging, dimly shining, blue python vines. Alada mewed softly, now touching the vines and looking up far into the canopy. "The trees may press in, but they steal the breath all the same."

She took a slow breath, trying to focus on beauty over unease.

Then — a voice. Indistinct, distant.

She froze.

Okay... I'm officially lost.

But when you're lost in the middle of a magical forest and you hear voices, you —?

You follow them.

"You know why I love the forest, Ember?" spoke the unknown voice.

Ember — he's here?! Alada thought.

"Coral, it's because I have so many friends!"

Coral too? Who are they even talking with? As Alada drew closer, she realized the speaker was none other than – "Tierra!" she mewed, stepping into a small clearing glowing with soft blue light.

"Alada! Oh! So glad you can be existing in this moment with us!" Tierra said in a somewhat misty voice while tumbling her over onto the soft ground with a tight hug, her green eyes shining like a kaleidoscope, reflecting the colors of the glowing forest.

"Ah yes," Alada coughed, lying sprawled on the ground, "I almost forgot how knocking the air out of someone is a feature of your hugs."

Tierra smiled, offering her a paw up.

"It's so marvelous to see you, but where are Ember and Coral?" Alada asked, dusting off her clothes.

"Over here," Tierra mewed as she leaped across the clearing and landed between two trees. "See? This is Ember," Tierra purred as she showed Alada a charred tree with a face carving of a very grumpy cat. "Ha! That's a good one! You know Ember these days — he's always cracking jokes. Am I right, Coral?" She motioned to the other oddly carved tree beside her.

Alada looked at Tierra somewhat nervously. "Right … um, I came here to chat a bit. Lately, I've been feeling lonely and—"

Tierra cut her off. "You know, when I'm feeling down, Jeff-tree *always* helps me feel better." Tierra motioned to a tree whose face was of a crudely carved, ugly bear — no, fish? Panda? Flamingo. "Yes, he is marvelous, isn't he?" Tierra said — as if she took *pride* in this monstrosity. "Jeff-tree aces every stop-quiz."

"Wait. *Stop*-quiz? You mean pop-quiz?" Alada asked, puzzled.

"You don't expect him to move *that* fast, do you? A tree that can *pop*?" She trailed off as she noticed the tightness in Alada's eyes. "Hey… you okay?"

Alada slightly nodded as Tierra measured her response.

"Well," Tierra said, finishing her thought, "I love art. Tierra — goddess and artist extraordinaire!"

Alada stared at her — she was lonely too — and then stared at her… tree art. She opened her mouth to comment, but her tummy grumbled noisily enough to fill the space where words would have been.

Tierra smiled, glancing over at Alada's belly. "I'm glad you came to see me. Loneliness is not something to joke around with."

Alada stared, silent and almost disbelieving.

"Okay, maybe I would, normally, but that's because I can

turn any situation into a joke. Another gift," said Tierra as Alada's belly made another churning grumble sound. She smiled. "Do you want something to eat?"

Alada grinned, unsure what to say.

"Come on, I'll show you where to find some maple cookies," Tierra said as she led Alada over to a particularly wide and twisted tree. "This tree leads to a grove where the Meus like to leave me my morning snack."

Alada stared at her. "How does that have anything to do with this tree?"

"Haven't you ever heard about, or done, tree traveling before? My gosh!" But Tierra didn't wait for a response and jumped into explaining what to do. "First, you listen and try to see if there's someone on the other side. Then, reach your paw though and—"

"Wait, I can't portal through trees like you," Alada objected. "That's quite the new ability you've built up since we last saw each other."

"Everyone can; it's just a matter of *your mind!*"

"Huh?"

"What I'm trying to say is that your thoughts are the only thing keeping you back. So, the key is believing in yourself!" Tierra mewed as she reached her upper body through the tree and came back with a basket of alsipreon needle tea, salty fish jerky, pomakee fruit jam with complimentary sundried leaf leathers, and an assortment of berryleaf fruits. "Do you want to share?"

"Yes, please, I'm starved!" Alada replied with an energetic purr.

"Do you want to go eat near the village?" Tierra asked. "The villagers are prepping for the cold winter season. It's fun to watch them."

"Yeah, okay. Sounds like fun, but how do we get there?"

"Through a tree," she answered casually.

Chapter 2
Hide and Find

Getting Alada to go through a tree was harder than it looked. First, she had the wings. "Tuck them in tight!"

"I *am* tucking them in tight!"

"You still have to breathe or it doesn't work right."

"How do you breathe in bark?"

"Okay, you're doing good. Just … beliiieeeve you can!"

"That's not heelllping!"

After that, it was a breeze … because Alada gave up and flew instead.

She found Tierra in the branches of an old-growth feather tree. It was her favorite napping spot, complete with a couple of feather-stuffed pillows. They perched high enough to watch the peaceful Meus go about their ordinary day and ordinary lives without being observed in return.

They ate in silence for a while until Tierra spoke, picking food with her claw from her teeth. "The Meus look so peaceful," she said, chewing again. "They've grown so much over the decades."

"Looks like there's a lot of them," Alada noted. "How big is this village?"

Tierra chewed and swallowed as quickly as possible. "A couple hundred Meus at this point. Their tree houses are fascinating. Oh! Oh!" Her tail fluffed as she stood, trying to get a better vantage point of something in the distance. "There's a temple dedicated to *me*! Do you want to see? Wanna see? They're so cool!" She jumped up and down, clasping her paws together in a relishing joy. "Partially designed by me." She put a paw on her chest, closing her eyes in pride.

"How?" Alada asked, giving her a raised eyebrow of you-know-better.

A sheepish expression filled Tierra's face. "Well, I … I gave them some prophecies, dreams," she coughed, "… omens and whatnot."

Alada continued with her flat expression.

"I am my own best high priestess." Tierra couldn't help but laugh at her own cleverness.

Alada shook her head, smiling all the same.

"After we finish eating, do you want to play a game?" Tierra asked.

"A game?"

"Yeah! In the fall, the Meus, aside from preparing for winter, play a large assortment of games or activities. It looks like Hide-and-Find is about to start!"

"What about our agreement? The oath we took?"

Tierra shamelessly stared into Alada's face without flinching. "I don't get mixed in their affairs. I go by a different name and just try to blend in as an ordinary Meu. They don't count on me for any aspect of these games. Wouldn't you go crazy if you didn't talk to anyone all these years?"

The blank stare on Alada's face, followed by her sad eyes, told Tierra all she needed to know. "Oh, Alada. Okay, that does it — you need to play right now. I didn't know you've literally been talking to *no one* all these years."

"It is super rare. I never thought to consider pretending to be someone else."

Tierra stood and bounded off toward the village. She could admit to herself that she sometimes played more than she should … even when the forest animals ran to her in fear, as they did now. Agitated squirrels nicked at her heels, chittering about a fire that had mysteriously ignited nearby. "If it's serious, it'll still be burning later," she mumbled, brushing them off. "Probably another camp fire or prescribed burn in another nearby village. Those squirrels..." *Every. Little. Thing. Decades in. Decades out.* She could hear the forest's warnings, but she was also really, really good at ignoring them. She didn't want to miss the game chasing what was probably just a little camp fire.

"You'll need a disguise," she said to Alada, ignoring the squirrels' pleas. She picked up two pawfulls of moss … and dirt … and threw them onto Alada, who looked down, mortified.

"What's that for?" Alada asked incredulously.

"You have to fit in. Now," Tierra said, touching her chin. "We need to do something about those wings."

Alada instinctively held her wings.

"Here." Tierra shoved a large-leaf backpack into her arms. "When you take mortal form, your wings will shrink, right?"

Alada's flat expression was more amusing than it should have been.

"You don't have to say anything," Tierra commented, as Alada clearly had no intention of explaining her wing transformation process. "Whether they shrink or fade or do some wing-magic thing, this backpack will help hide them either way."

Tierra could clearly hear telepathic messages from the distressed animals and trees from a nearby part of the forest, but was simultaneously experiencing her own deep longing as she thought of the starting game. *But this* is *my favorite game! ... Okay, they're* all *my favorite game ... Yeah, the forest can take care of itself. I'm sure it's nothing,* Tierra reasoned. A twinge filled her stomach and then a horn sounded, echoing in the trees.

She looked at Alada's dirt and mud splotches. "That'll do," she stated as she grabbed Alada's hand, practically dragging her through the forest toward the village. All the while, she told her of all the rules, though she wondered if Alada could actually hear all of them as they bushwhacked through to a trail.

"Tierra, just to confirm, the game is: half of the village

hides, including me, and the other half, including you, go around finding the hiders. Once hiders are found, they have to return to the village. And the last one to be found in each age category wins a prize or two, and the finders who find the most cats get prizes too."

"Practically word for word!" Tierra stammered at her memory.

They meandered over to a clearing where Meus gathered. Referees were walking around announcing the rules while reminding newer cats of the spectator's non-interference clause.

Alada could barely feel her paws beneath her. The feeling — so full, so warm, so unlike the ache of loneliness — nearly brought her to tears. It had been ages since she'd been surrounded by villagers. Any villagers of any nation. She couldn't help smiling to herself, even though she still didn't fully comprehend how taking on an undercover identity didn't go against their oaths as Guardians.

"Is everyone ready?" the referee called out.

"Yes!" cheered the crowd.

"Of course, now let's start already!" called some kittens.

Cats cheered from all around the clearing as everyone took their places: finders in the center together with hiders spaced out along the rim. Alada stood near some kittens who were already talking about their hiding spots, noisily. Tierra stood in the middle with the other finders, facing inward, chatting animatedly.

"Then, on that note," said the referee, reaching into his

mushroom-leather bag and pulling out a bottle. Upon uncorking, smoke poured out the top in a thick, foggy, and dull blue mist.

I love this part, Tierra thought. The dull blue fog swirled around her ankles and encompassed her body as it filled the clearing. She heard paws scampering into the trees, as cats ran for cover before the five-minute mist dissipated. She took this time to ponder where Alada might hide. *Maybe she'll hide in that hallowed out tree? Or maybe with her big wings, she'll cram into that glowing bush … but she probably wouldn't with all those python vines in the way.* She smiled and began stretching her paws. *It won't be that hard to find her. She won't bother trying to climb into the trees anyway. They're too thick, so that's just one less place to look.*

The second the fog fully cleared, Tierra dashed into the trees and instantly found three Meus — not by sight though. Being the 911 of the forest had its perks. She could hear, telepathically, from the trees and plants as they were being overrun with a kingdom of hiding cats.

She dashed up to the nearest cat with spotted green fur (well-hidden in a hollow log) and tagged him with a victorious grin.

Next, she found a bluish Meu awkwardly wedged into a rabbit's den. Tierra reached in and tapped her tail.

Then she spotted a third — a sleek tabby perched on a low branch of a bushy alsipreon tree. Tierra leapt up and tagged her gently on the lower back. The she-cat shrieked and flailed, losing her balance.

Chapter 2

WHUMP!

She toppled backward, landing directly on Tierra's chest and knocking the air from her lungs. "*Oof!* Surprise pounce. Bold move," Tierra coughed, "I respect that," she wheezed, blinking at the sky.

The Meu scrambled back onto her paws, saying, "I'm so, so, *so* sorry about falling on you! You're so quiet! I did not expect to be found so soon." The she-cat's eyes drifted over Tierra's shoulder, noticing the two other found cats waiting to return to the clearing. "You've already found *three* of us?"

Suddenly, the green spotted cat shouted, "All right, Falcor! Let's stop wasting that seeker's time. She has cats to find!"

"Okay, sorry 'bout that. I wish you luck!" Falcor called back to Tierra as she and the other two cats padded off toward the starting area.

Hiding cats were blooming in wild flower patches and insulating hollowed logs and trees. Fur seemed to be everywhere Tierra looked! Every few paces, she spotted fur or a tail just out of the corner of her eye. This wasn't surprising though given her telepathic powers. What was most surprising wasn't the Meu who'd fallen on her, nor even that Alada had turned up in her little clearing this morning — it was the fact that she had not found Alada yet.

She padded on for a few more minutes until she spotted the tip of a tail coming from beneath the bushes surrounding an old alsipreon tree. She trotted toward the tail, ready to tag— *Thump!* —only to bump into another cat heading for the same target. The tail from under the bush swept completely under as if the hider pulled itself into a ball.

Tierra stared at the cat she'd bumped into, uncertain who would get the point for tagging this target. The male cat stared, puzzled, as if thinking the same thing.

"How about you take the point? I have plenty," Tierra offered.

The male cat's eyes perked up. "Thanks! Are you sure? We were both equally close."

Tierra shrugged. "No, it's okay. You–"

They heard a loud sneeze from the nearby bush. They turned as the bush shook. From inside came a high-pitched voice: "Ah, man! Now I'm sure to be found!" The male cat walked up to the bush, using his paws to pull back the branches. Inside the center sat a small moss-colored cat no older than six. He waved at the kitten and said, "Found you! Do you want me to bring you back to the clearing? You're pretty far off."

"No. I is brave." The little boy kitten straightened up tall, put back his shoulders and marched off with his bravest walk.

"I'm Birch," he said, turning back to Tierra. He had orange fur with cream-colored stripes on his face and down his neck. His sap-green eyes were rather striking. "I've seen you before. Nice to meet you, Holly."

Holly? Tierra blinked. She was just about to correct him—then remembered her pseudonym. "Right, yes. Of course. I'm Holly. Nice to meet you too, Birch."

Chapter 2

They started to part ways when a different solid-green cat bounded over. "There's only one cat left! You better keep an eye out!"

Tierra's eyes widened. "Wait — already?"

"Yeah, I know. This game has been going much faster these past few years. More cats, more finders," Birch said as the other finder ran off.

Tierra nodded. "Well, good luck to you!" She scampered off. *He seems like a nice guy.*

Even with luck on her side, the game had just gotten harder. Seekers ran around, climbing the low branches of trees, looking anywhere they could, trying to find the last hider. *Who could hide so well that* this *many cats can't find him or her? Speaking of* her, *I wonder who ended up finding Alada?* Despite this curiosity, she refocused. *Gotta win. Gotta focus. I wish those squirrels and their silly fire would stop interrupting the trees from giving me the location of this hider extraordinaire!* She paused. *Unless I already passed them.*

Chapter 3
Finding Alada

Looking around, the forest appeared practically empty, except for a few finders still poking around, either determined to win or losing a bet. In any case, they might as well give up because she was going to beat *all* of them with *all* of their points put together.

Tierra poked her head into the last hollowed-out log in the area, squinted her eyes as she looked around, but found nothing … again. *Perhaps they tried to hide up high?* She bent her legs and leaped onto the nearest tree branch, and started climbing up its trunk with her claws extended. *Ready or not, here I come.* As she reached the top of the canopy, she shouted, "Aha! Found you…?" She felt her own face fall as she gazed over the sea of trees with no one to be found.

She groaned noisily, looking all around when something dark caught her eye. A cloud of midnight-black smoke was rising in the distance. Guilt tugged at her stomach. *This is what they were warning me about…*

A small voice sounded from behind her. "Notice it too?"

Tierra turned — surprised at the fact that someone was behind her. Perched atop a tree was a she-cat with cloud-white fur. Her once-pristine golden top and cream-colored pants were now smeared with dirt and dotted with crumbly moss, while her large feathered wings were tangled with twigs. She was gazing at Tierra with wide, worried blue eyes that mirrored the sky. As the smoke increased, her eyes grew grayer by the minute.

Ash sprinkled through the air like snowflakes, and a pungent waft of smoke stung their noses.

Tierra reached out, tapped her on the shoulder, and said with a small smile, "Found you, Alada."

"We should investigate," Alada said as she urgently climbed down the tree.

"Wait now! Even though the fires seem like the biggest problem, it would be much worse if we also had one hundred Meus searching for us. We would just end up leading them into the center of danger in their search."

"So, how long do we have to get back before they come looking for us?" came Alada's voice from just below the canopy.

"Nine minutes."

"Think we could walk back to the clearing in time?"

"No."

Claws on bark scratched loudly as Alada poked her head back up, clearly puzzled. "Then how do we get back in time?"

"Tree traveling!" Tierra exclaimed as she threw her paws up, shaking them — jazz-hands style.

"Ah, great…" Alada sighed.

Another whiff of smoke curled through the air — sharp and sudden as if a message of urgency from the forest itself.

Chapter 4

An Unpleasant Surprise

Imagine being shoved though a wall of sap, not meta-phorically, but literally. And that, my friend, is tree traveling.

"Don't worry, the more you do it, the less sticky it gets!" Tierra said as she swayed with the plants behind her.

"Ya-huh, sure," Alada replied while she attempted to lick off the sap stuck to her wings, which, to her dismay, did not taste like syrup. "How do you get this stuff off?"

"I haven't worried about sap in a while, but something I remember doing was sitting in super-hot water while con-sistently licking."

"Is there a way without becoming cat broth?"

"Well … you could wait until it hardens, jump off a cliff, and see if it breaks?"

Alada's flat expression lingered.

"Okay, I don't *actually* remember," Tierra admitted with a shrug. "But I bet someone in the village will. We can ask one of the medicine cats after the game." She began to saunter off toward the village. "Now, speaking of priorities…"

"Fine … you're right. I can get this off later."

Alada followed Tierra through the various shrubs and bushes, with branches, buds, flowers, bristles, cones, leaves, twigs, and various pine needles sticking to her fur as she passed.

Once Tierra turned around near the village, she couldn't help but stare and marvel. "Woah! Alada! I'm not gonna lie — this is a way better disguise than the mud and moss. We should've gotten you stuck in sap earlier! You're a genius!" Tierra cheered, already marching ahead. "I don't remember you getting into games this much before. This is just what you needed!" she called back over her shoulder.

Stiffening as she walked, Alada kept muted as she marched toward the village, all while collecting enough wilderness materials to host a build-your-own deluxe nesting event.

As they approached the clearing, cheers erupted as a crowd of Meus rushed toward them with treats and prizes in their arms.

"You get the reward for finding the most cats!" one referee announced to Tierra as another Meu shoved a container of popple milk in her arms.

"Wait—" Alada started. She needed to tell them about the smoke.

"And you get the award for finding the most cats in ten minutes," the referee continued toward Tierra.

"Thank you, but we—" Tierra said.

"And, you get the award for finding the most prestigious

hiders."

"As all would expect," Tierra said, grinning, taking the trophy.

"And, you get the award for finding the first three hiders!"

"Not bad, I would say." She perked her ears up.

Alada hissed sharply to regain her attention.

"You, of course, also get the reward for finding the last three hiders," the referring continued, pouring gifts into Tierra's arms.

"Oh, well, it was nothing," Tierra replied, again losing sight of her mission.

"We need your attention!" Alada snapped through tightly pursed lips. Each step and movement tugged more fur from her body and face, the gluey sap turning every movement into a slow-motion hair removal treatment.

"Yes! You do!" exclaimed the referee as he turned his attention to her. "You get the prize for hiding at the highest elevation!"

"What?" Alada said.

"You get the prize for hiding the longest!"

"Thank you, but—"

"You get the prize for being the dirtiest hider!"

"*That's a prize?*"

The other Meus tried to shove prizes into her arms, but they were so covered in leaves and debris that she couldn't hold anything ... so they stuck the prizes to the outsides of her arms.

"And you get the award for finding the five youngest hiders," the referee said, returning his focus to Tierra.

"Wow, really?"

"You get the award for finding the eldest hider."

"Who was that?"

"It was me! Grandpa!" said a bright, cheerful, and energetic Meu with one gray stripe on his beard.

"I have a grandpa?"

"He's everyone's grandpa," the referee said, holding out a trophy with a long bearded elder cat on it.

"We need to tell you something!" Alada exclaimed as loudly as she could over the hustle and bustle of the award announcements and prize exchanges.

"This year," the referee announced to the village, turning his back on Alada and Tierra, "we have a tie for first place!"

"What?!" Tierra choked out. Her tail puffed into a bristling plume, ears flattening against her head. Her pupils narrowed to angry slits as the words echoed in her skull. A tie? That couldn't be right. She never tied.

"Holly and Birch!"

Birch bounded over, radiant. "Isn't this exciting? We're tied!"

Tierra didn't blink. Her jaw tightened. Her claws flexed around her prizes like they might disintegrate under pressure. "Ecstatic," she said in a voice that could curdle milk.

"Ecstatic, indeed!" Birch cheered, bouncing in place as his prizes and trophies jostled and nearly spilled. "And Holly, you said you were the best ever!"

Tierra's arms clenched her winnings even tighter, and the

sound of her claws scraping the metal trophies screeched lightly. "Con … congratulations."

"We're like a team! You find half, and I find the other. No one will be found unless by us!" Birch gave a cheerful chuckle, but glanced away a beat too fast—like he suddenly wasn't sure Tierra saw it the same way.

Alada, watching closely, could tell: Birch was overjoyed. Tierra was not. And if Tierra didn't want her hard-earned prizes crushed into glittering confetti, someone had better intervene.

"Oh, hello," Alada said quickly, stepping forward with an overly polite smile. "You're Birch, right? The one who tied with Tier—sorry—Holly?"

Birch blinked and turned toward her. "Huh? Oh, yes! And you must be FurAhLees—the last one to be found, right?"

"FurAh-wha?"

Tierra shot her a warning glance. Alada rolled her eyes and scowled back, knowing this was the random pseudonym Tierra must have given her.

"Yes, of course, I'm … Fur-ay-knees."

Birch seemed satisfied and bounded off, with bottles of flower milk, soups, and treats trailing behind him.

Alada turned back towards Tierra. "Curry Flees. Really?"

"Not *Curry Flees,* nor *FurAyKnees,* or *Furry Bees,* it's FurAhLees! It's not that hard!"

"Something else that wouldn't be too hard is you quitting the Undercover Name Creating Industry — the U.N.C.I.

for short."

"Is that a real industry?"

"No."

"Then how— you know what? Never mind. I won't ask," Tierra muttered, flicking an ear in mild irritation. She paused, nostrils flaring. "That's... a potent smell."

She sniffed again. "Smells like the air current changed. Smoke. Maybe something drifted in from the fire pits. Or—" Her voice trailed off as her pupils shrank. "Do you have a hose? I should probably—"

She didn't finish.

Alada had gone still. Her gaze locked with Tierra's for one, heartbeat-long moment—then she bolted.

She didn't make it far.

Two steps forward and the truth hit like a wall: the entire perimeter of the village was smoldering. Smoke rose in pillars from every direction, curling into the sky like tendrils. A red-orange glow licked the trunks of the outer trees. Alada froze. All around her, shrieks shattered the afternoon air.

Behind her—*clang!* Tierra's trophies hit the ground.

She didn't move. She didn't blink. Her ears had flattened against her skull.

Alada turned. Tierra was staring straight into the fire's glow, her body rigid, jaw tight, fur bristling.

The game was over.

"What do we do?" Alada breathed, too quietly to be heard by any normal ear.

Only Tierra's eyes moved to look at her. "I've built a life

with these Meus. I can't leave them to the fire. We can't leave. We can use our powers to save them."

Alada shook her head. "If we use too much of our strength and powers, they'll know it's us. You'd never be able to come back … *for generations.*"

Alada could sense the dread of isolation in Tierra's eyes.

"Decide," Tierra said. There was no time for anything but a decision. "Help or don't help. We weren't meant to help in smaller squabbles, but we can."

"Fine," Alada stated. "We'll help, but we won't use our full strength and power. We will help as we can — as Holly and FurryKnees." She looked down at her sap-covered body. "Good lot of help I'll be…"

Tierra clapped a paw on her sticky shoulder, though struggled slightly to remove it. "Well, we'll make it work."

Then came the screams—louder this time. Not from one place, but from everywhere.

They turned as a sudden whoosh of flame burst upward, devouring the far edge of the village. A wall of fire raged where buildings had stood only seconds before. Trees cracked and fell, the heat licking outward with unnatural speed.

The villagers had no way out.

"How is it spreading that fast?" Tierra asked, her voice tight, her ears twitching back in alarm. "That's not normal."

"No," Alada said, eyes narrowing. "It's not."

They saw a figure behind the flames—like a shadow within the fire itself—its paw outstretched as if willing the blaze to swell and burn hotter.

No matter where the villagers tried to run, hide, or flee—the fire was already there, roaring through every exit.

And now, what is that?

Dark, hulking creatures emerged through the flames unharmed, as if fire welcomed them. They had thin, pointed ears, elongated snouts, and broad, muscular shoulders. Their shadowy hides seemed to drink in the light, making their armor blend almost seamlessly into the smoke.

Glowing eyes cut through the haze. Clawed feet crushed embers beneath them with slow, deliberate strides, leaving scorched tracks behind.

Before Alada or Tierra could even decide how to help, every able-bodied Meu raced for the hidden armories—hollowed within ancient trees and concealed behind bark-like doors.

With barely a word exchanged, dozens of Meus emerged with staffs and swords in paw. More followed by the minute, pouring from the tree-bunkers like a living surge of defiance. They charged toward beasts twice their size in every direction.

Alada's mouth dropped open as she watched three Meus attacking a single creature, yet with all their might, it did all but nothing to drive the beast back to the flames.

One of the beasts stalked toward a mother shielding a cluster of kittens in the center of the clearing.

Alada's blood surged. She couldn't stop herself — not this time. She sprinted forward, sap clinging to her limbs, slowing every step. As she ran, she snatched a wooden staff from a fallen warrior.

The cries of the kittens echoed in Alada's ears.

We must save the kittens. How do I do it? She looked around, but the fire sealed off all exits. Visions of flying came to mind, but she couldn't break cover over a single fight. No matter how they all cried, she couldn't fly them to safety. She felt a tear stream down her face as the sounds of metal against wood clanged in her ears. *The kittens. How do I save them?*

As the creature's sword descended upon the protective mother, his blade collided with the back of Alada's wings — *crack!* She turned around sharply, with the blade still stuck, having wrenched it from his hands, while hitting him squarely across the face with her staff.

With her back now facing the mother, who wrenched the blade free for her own use, now shielded the kittens from another angle. The kittens began throwing rocks, pummeling the thing's face.

"Graah!" the beast growled, shielding its face with its arms, unintentionally leaving the rest of itself unguarded, an opportunity the mother used to start hacking at the creature's feet with her new extra-sharp sword.

Alada stepped aside, holding the creature's gaze. *Move away from the kittens. Follow me.* It worked. "Stand down!" she commanded, distancing herself from the kittens.

The creature merely exhaled a rather chuckle-ish snort. "No interest in kittens," it growled and grunted, "But plenty in you." It barred its teeth again, showing his sharp fangs. He took one last glance at the mother behind her, who hissed menacingly.

"Stand down," Alada commanded again, holding her staff at the ready.

Once again, it mildly chuckled. "No." He stepped forward, swinging his fist blindingly fast, and grabbed the staff in one quick swipe. Instantly, he broke it in half with one squeeze. "No," it said more loudly. "NO!" it roared again, stepping forward yet again.

She turned and darted several yards away; she could hear his grunts to keep up. *It's working.* "You think *you* can take *me* on, you—" she said. *Tierra's much better at trash-talking.* "…you mangey, smelly, fool!" she yelled.

It stopped — momentarily amused, but got over itself quickly. "*BOLD WORDS,* CAT!" he growled louder than ever before.

"You don't know what I'm capable of!"

He grinned, showing every tooth, his mouth dripping with saliva. "Who cares? I'll have your pelt in one swipe if I want it."

Still backing up, Alada didn't realize she had been backing up right against a tree. *Oh, no.* The creature charged with both arms into her shoulders, pressing the sap on her back deep into all the tree's bark. *Crack.* Pain flared up in her chest, and too dazed by the impact to react, she slumped back against the tree, pain swelling inside her.

He chuckled low and cold, as if delighting in her helplessness. "Watch it burn," he whispered—each word dripping with malicious intent.

He paused, letting his laughter—half growl, half jeer—linger in the air. Then he turned and strode straight into the panicked crowd of Meus. Exhaustion painted their faces as they struggled upright, and he lunged at them like a predator smelling fear.

All she could do was watch.

The first thing that caught her eye was Tierra lunging at a creature with a double-pointed staff — but the creature was disappearing? *No,* Alada thought. The beast vanished mid-swing — not invisibly, but with a shimmering snap, the air folding in on itself like a curtain yanked aside and then dropped. He reappeared several feet away, snarling. *Glitching,* Alada realized — a warped kind of teleportation, raw and unnatural. She'd seen teleportation before — this wasn't that. This was messy. Broken. The creature glitched instantly out of existence every time a swing came at it, and then returned to deliver its own blow.

Then she spotted Birch.

To her surprise, he was still standing — not just standing, but darting around like he'd trained for this. He clutched one of his oversized trophies like a club, the golden base reflecting firelight as he weaved between strikes. He ducked, rolled, and sidestepped with sharp instincts and a surprising amount of speed.

He didn't land a single blow.

But it didn't matter — not yet. He was staying alive.

Alada felt a spark of hope.

Then, in an instant, the beast adjusted. It faked left, glitched right, and Birch's foot slipped on a patch of scorched earth. He barely had time to raise his trophy before the creature swatted it away and slammed the flat of its blade into his side.

Birch flew backward, crashing into a bed of overgrown button lilac. Petals and ash erupted into the air.

Alada's breath caught, but no one turned to check on him. Everyone was fighting, barely holding ground.

Alada heard Tierra's infamous hiss-screech that came with growing frustration. She was a seasoned swordscat but still hadn't landed a single hit. Further surveying her surroundings, Alada realized that there were no fallen beasts, only Meus. She saw Tierra use her spear to pole-vault onto the beast's head, but in a flash of glitch, she passed straight through his body, landing hard.

When the beast appeared again, Tierra sliced it across his belly with her staff. Alada watched as the beast glitched on the first impact — but not fast enough to dodge the second. Her claws struck moments after the staff — slashing deep across its face. The beast stumbled back, with a wide-eyed appearance of horror. Clearly, it hadn't expected any hits to land, and it touched its face, now full of blood from the gaping cuts. As Tierra lined up for another attack, the beast glitched out of existence.

Tierra stood frozen for a moment before frantically looking all around to see if the beast would reappear beside her, behind her — anywhere. But it didn't. Still, there was no time to think as she joined the nearest Meu against its beast, but again, the creature glitched out, leaving her to stare at the equally confused eyes of the referee, his flank now covered in his own blood.

The screams faltered. One by one, voices fell silent.

And then… nothing.

A strange hush blanketed the battlefield. The fire still cracked. The trees still smoldered. But every Meu stood motionless, exchanging wide-eyed stares, uncertain if the creatures had truly vanished or were simply hiding somewhere nearby. No one moved. No one spoke.

Then Tierra exhaled sharply — a shuddering breath — and broke the silence. "Grandpa! Can you help me move the injured off the ground?" she called, her voice firm despite the trembling in her limbs. She bounded toward him as he bent to lift a spotted green cat struggling to stand.

Still stuck to the tree, Alada realized that the once roaring ring of fire had swiftly died down to a few flickering flames and embers. *How could a fire start that fast and almost completely stop in a matter of minutes? One thing is for sure — that was magic, and that figure in the flames we saw before the beasts appeared had something to do with it.*

Chapter 5

The Phantom

F ine work," the black-hooded figure said, by no means a compliment.

The black cat lightly hissed. "It was nothing. The worst part was trying to keep the bulk of the smoke out of their—" the cat motioned to some beasts who were badly playing chess, "—drooly snouts."

The beasts growled at the insult but soon went back to their game — pawns hopping over bishops, horses diagonally attacking pieces, and the king and queen's abilities swapped. One beast knocked a queen off the board with a pawn. "Tag, you're it!"

"Be patient with these stupid, drool-faced beasts." A deep, resonant chuckle echoed in the room. "Try not to get too far on their bad side. They can still kill you."

The beasts nodded in agreement.

The black cat hissed with a large roll of his eyes. "If they don't mind a face-full of fire first."

"You know you can't hit them. No one can."

"No? Someone did!" One beast stood up, displaying a large wound full of dried blood on the side of its face.

The cloaked figure turned his attention to the deep gashes across the beast's face, but did not care to look closer. "Serves you right."

The beast growled as he sat back down.

"I'm honored your knees are too weak to stand before me, beast, but tell me who did this … if you can remember that far back."

Again, the beast looked up, growling deep in his throat. "A Meu with a staff."

"They all had staffs," the black cat said, mockingly.

The beast barked loudly, ending with a menacing growl. "This one was just slightly faster than the rest."

"More like *you* were *slower,* and it just caught you off guard," the black cat spat.

"No, it was—"

"Report to training. Two weeks should be enough to drill it into your thick, single-celled brain. Then you can rejoin the ranks." The cloaked figure sighed with obvious disapproval. "Now be gone with you."

The beast lowered its head in shame. "Yes, master," it said, then glitched out.

"Ugh … these mutts take forever to teach!" The black cat sighed.

"Ignorant, know-it-all fur balls," the master said.

The black cat glared at the figure in the cloak and glitched out.

Tierra almost let go of her double-edged staff—just like every other Meu—when the attackers simply vanished. One blink, and they were gone. No smoke trail. No retreat. Just… gone.

From the brush nearby, Birch staggered out, clutching his now-battered trophies like a child might cling to safety blankets. Dents marked their edges. His fur was singed and dusted in ash.

"You survived by wielding trophies?" Tierra asked, half in disbelief, half in admiration, leaning on her staff.

Birch didn't answer. He only stared at her, wide-eyed, and shifted his weight with uncertainty.

A pause passed between them.

"I am impressed," she said at last, softer this time. Her smile was faint, but real.

Birch blinked, surprised by the praise. Then he nodded once and darted off to help another Meu carry the wounded from the charred battlefield.

"Respectfully, slowly. Let's set the bodies in a line so we know exactly how many honor shrouds the death doulas need to make. We need to set up the Honor ceremony as soon as possible," Tierra heard Birch say as he grunted with the weight of the fallen.

She turned her focused attention on the rest of the villagers, whom were now helping the wounded and soothing the scared. Then she saw Alada leaning against a tree on the edge of the clearing. She scampered over and as she drew closer, saw that she wasn't pleasantly leaning against the tree … but was actually stuck a few inches off the ground, hanging from the sap still on her wings and back. "Are you okay?" she called, examining the level of stuckness, which was a ten out of ten.

Alada's furrowed brows and crossed arms said it all. She sighed. "If you're unwilling to assist me, then fetch another who will."

"It'll be okay. I'll be right back," Tierra said as she walked briskly over to the nearest medicine cat, which happened to be Falcor.

As Tierra padded up to her, Falcor jumped a little, looking over her shoulder with nervous, wide eyes, but was relieved to see who it was.

"Oh, it's just you, Holly. I was worried the beasts had come back!"

"Yes, well, thank Tierra that didn't happen! Anyway, Jury Keys got stuck to a tree. Can you help her out?"

"Okay, sure, just hand me some of that Sap Dissolvent. It's in the large bottle to your right of the medicine bag."

Tierra pointed to a blue dyed moss pouch.

"Yes, that one on the ground. That should be enough to get her free. Then we can get the rest off later."

Tierra stood, stunned. "How long have we had that?!"

Falcor stared at her, confused. "Umm, about a century, I think."

"Huh! The years just fly by, don't they?"

"… I think I'm … going to go help Hurry Please," Falcor said before she ran off.

Was it something I said? Tierra thought. She walked off toward a group of Meus who were wandering in and out of burnt structures, trying to salvage and clean as they went. *What a mess.*

She caught sight of Birch feeding some kittens the sweet milk he had won just before the attack. She felt a sweet flutter in her heart. *How thoughtful. Genuine kindness.*

Birch turned around from feeding the kittens fish crackers. "Hey, Holly, do you want to play with the kittens and I? I'm trying to lighten the mood." He rubbed a smudge of ash from his cheek. "When I was their age, I thought the worst thing that could happen was losing a game. Let's give them a bit of that world back, just for today."

"Sure," Tierra said as she padded up to Birch and the small crowd of little Meus. "What do you all want to play?"

"Moss ball!"

"Hide and Find!"

"RAID!"

Tierra tilted her head. "What's that game?"

A spotted tree-green she-kitten replied, "It's one I just made up. You two," she pointed to Tierra and Birch, "are the beasts — the big, scary kind you just fought. And the rest of us will be the warriors who'll beat you!"

Birch and Tierra exchanged looks and came to an agreement.

"How about moss ball? That sound fun," Birch said.

"Hoo-way!" one extra small Meu exclaimed.

"Okay, who's wants to fetch a ball?"

"ME, ME, ME!" all the kittens shouted as they all ran off.

Birch and Tierra stood there, waiting for the kittens to retrieve a ball. They waited silently and listened to the passing villagers as they'd walk by:

"I can't believe this happened."

"Did anyone see how they appeared?"

"How did the fire even start? I didn't see a torch. Did you?"

"How many Meus are injured?"

"Are all the kittens safe?"

"Maybe there was an explosion. Or maybe a dragon?"

"Aren't those just in myths?"

Just then, all the kittens ran toward them, each carrying a ball.

"I found one!"

"Use mine!"

"How awesome," Tierra said. "How *amazing* that we get to use one ball and have two extras in case we need it."

Alada approached from behind. "Sweet kittens," she said. She was leaning heavily on a tall stick and had a bandage wrapped around her head.

"Oof, what happened to you? Did you decide to jump off the cliff?" Tierra teased.

Alada responded by glaring at her, then turned her attention back to the kittens. "Playing moss ball?"

Birch nodded his head. "Indeed! Would you want to join, Murry Sneeze?"

Alada stared at him blankly. "Call me Jasmine. FurAhlees is my *middle* name." She looked at Tierra pointedly.

Tierra shrugged in response.

Birch blushed. "Sorry, Scurey Mes— I mean … Jasmine."

Alada looked satisfied enough, then took one of the moss balls, tossing it as high as she could to start the game, which was quite high considering she had obviously broken a bone or two (though it would heal within an hour or so).

The moment she threw the ball upward, the oldest kitten sprung atop Birch's shoulders and leapt up and off him to catch it, knocking Birch hard to the ground before subsequently landing on his chest.

"I caught it!" the kitten mewed with delight.

Birch staggered to his feet. "Wonderful, now, how 'bout you guys keep playing over there—" he pointed away towards a not so distant tree, "while we stay here and talk about *boring* grown-up stuff."

The kittens looked a bit disappointed, but still bounded off to play.

"What is this '*boring* grown-up stuff' you speak of?" Tierra said.

"Well, the fight of course!"

"… I wouldn't consider that boring … just—"

"Nightmarish?" Alada suggested.

"Intense," Tierra and Birch said at once.

"Ah." Alada agreed.

Birch bent down, picking up a burned chunk of wood from the ground, turning it slowly in his paw. "We'll rebuild," he said softly. "But I'd rather know who we're rebuilding against." He turned and looked toward a group of slow-moving Meus gathering together in a huddle. "Looks like a meeting is about to start, so we should join in," Birch said as he strode off.

Alada watched him walk off, uncertain if she and Tierra should follow. "Should we join him?"

"Yes, we should be there to give our input on the battle," Tierra replied, padding over to where Birch went.

Alada momentarily hesitated, looking back towards the three kittens playing by the tree, then hurried off to join Tierra.

In the center of a sizeable crowd of Meus, an old Meu (not older than Grandpa, mind you) shouted, "All the houses are nothing but ash!"

"Where did they come from?" another cried out.

"They just appeared!" the game referee called out. "Appeared out of flame!"

"They didn't come from the flame," an old grandma corrected.

"How can you be so sure?"

The grandma shrugged.

"It was the fire first!" called Birch. "I saw a light first."

"How many beasts were there? Was anyone able to estimate?" called one of the town elders, now covered in ash, soot and dapples of dried blood.

"Who had time to estimate?" said a mother, loudly. "We were protecting ourselves and our loved ones."

Alada recognized the mother and her kittens. The mother was only holding two now, though she had been protecting many more.

"They were all scattered. It was hard to tell," Birch called out. "But based on my experience, I'd say two or three to one are the general odds. These beasts could certainly handle more than one of us at a time." He looked over to Tierra, whom he had seen handle a beast all on her own, but she was the only one who had done so beside himself and the few village warriors they had.

Soft yells in the distance suddenly came closer as the kittens who were playing with the ball raced toward everyone in attendance. "Quick!" they all mewed one after the other.

Scoffs of annoyance from a couple older Meus echoed, but the urgency of the kittens had most everyone paying attention, and they started following the kittens toward the forest beyond the clearing, leaving the scoffers behind.

Through the thicket of bushes and trees, they came upon a small clearing of large boulders that generations of kittens had pounced, climbed, and jumped upon. The kittens didn't jump or climb them now, but stood at the foot of the 20-foot compilation of rocks and boulders.

The village elders made their way from the back of the group through hushed murmurs and bouts of hisses. When the last of the villagers spread to make space before the great boulders, the village elders beheld a sight that brought an unnatural cold into their bodies.

Before them, scorched into the largest boulder, was a

message like a scar: YOU ARE NOW UNDER THE COMMAND OF THE PHANTOM.

The villagers murmured amongst themselves as to not frighten the kittens with hisses and screeches and screams.

The elders each took a turn to look and Moss, the eldest elder, approached, trying to brush the ash away, but the letters wouldn't smudge. "We will not be dominated. We bow to none other than Gata de la Tierra!" He tried again, but his efforts cleaned the rock, making the letters stand out more.

"Is it scratched in?" Tierra whispered. "It looks burned into the stone — as if the fire had carved it with teeth."

Moss and the others immediately retreated through the aisle, back to the village.

Tierra and Alada looked at each other. Alada, though, couldn't shake a deep feeling — as if the words themselves stood guard — silent sentinels of a power yet unseen.

"Who's the P-han-tom?" asked one villager.

"What's a pantom?" asked another.

"A type of dog?"

"Maybe a bird?"

"Why would a bird try to control us?" hollered Grandpa. "We'd just eat it, anyway. In my day, we ate anything that tried to control us. First there were the squirrels with their nut helmets and matchbox chariots..."

Tierra smiled, remembering those days. Remembering when Grandpa was a little whippersnapper. Yet, she said nothing. She loved listening to him, no matter what age.

The entire village sat or stood with quiet respect as Grandpa spoke.

"Then there were the ants! Boy, the ant army was the worst! We called in all the birds in the area to help with that! Then, of course, there were the winter rabbits and their carrot raids in the darkness of night!"

Tierra noticed Alada looking at her out the corner of her eye.

"Then there were the glowing lizards. Now, those things were monsters! So, we found a happy equilibrium with them creatures. They guard our gardens in exchange for…"

She nudged Alada to follow her and they quietly dismissed themselves from the crowd. They tiptoed away to the sounds of Grandpa reminiscing. They waited to be entirely alone before talking, yet Tierra only whispered.

"Strange," Tierra said.

"Sounds like this happens all the time," Alada said, "according to Grandpa."

Tierra smirked. She felt a swelling in her chest when she thought of that old cat. "He wasn't even around for the glowing lizards," she said, laughing a little. "But — something is wrong. This is different. Much different."

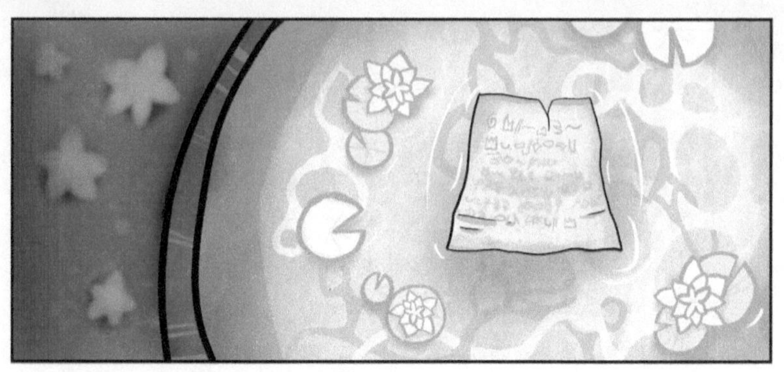

Chapter 6

Aftermath

Alada agreed. This felt familiar – long, long ago familiar. So long ago, that the memories felt fuzzy and unclear.

Tierra sighed heavily. "Meus are great in so many ways, and they are also skilled at growing produce! The rabbits, ants, and the squirrels — the lizards were a bit different — they all just wanted a bite. But this? No, no, no. This was a full-fledged burning RAID!" Tierra stood clenching her fists, her eyes glowing with rage. Tierra paused before she continued speaking, but Alada cut her off.

"Why do the villagers seem so … how do I put it? Calm. I mean, just look." Alada motioned over to the villagers who seemed to be quickly getting over their shock what with the adults cleaning up, the kittens playing with balls — re-enacting the fight, mothers cuddling their littles, she-cats passing out food. There were no tears, crying, or screaming. Alada continued, "If they are fine, so are we, right?"

"The Meus are the most connected to nature and Source.

They don't see death and destruction in quite the same way. While they do mourn, and they will, their understanding of the afterlife exceeds even my own, I think." Tierra looked at her, her eyes growing brighter. "Let's still provide the elders our perspective."

"With that, I agree." Alada stood, prompting Tierra to lead the way to elders.

"The things appeared from the flames!" one elder argued.

"And them beasts kept teleportin' away from me swipes!" another said.

"How did they move so fast?" asked a village warrior, Bramble. His arm bandages fell askew and soon fell to the ground as he moved around. "I couldn't land a single strike."

"But they sure landed a ton. The count of fallen is at twenty and rising," said Moss, an elder who wore a moss-covered headdress decorated with bioluminescent sponges, lichen, and mushrooms. He sat on a large, charred stump. The smell of smoldering, burnt wood lingered in the air. "And to think this was an entire tree," he said, motioning to his stump-chair. "No one had a good enough look to see what happened."

No one spoke as it was true. No villagers had seen what had happened. Alada noticed, however. She noticed that they glitched while fighting, like static, and then glitched right out of existence.

No clue where they went, Alada thought. *Did they glitch*

somewhere or just …? "We need to tell them what we saw," Alada whispered to Tierra, who shook her head in response. "I thought we agreed!"

"No, now I feel we should try to keep them out of this as much as possible."

"They're already in it. They need to know the true danger," Alada insisted.

"I don't want them getting harmed trying to face this threat. We need them to know that they need to lie low, under the activity radar. That includes the other smaller villages in the forest."

"We need to go warn as many of the bigger villages as possible. The bigger ones can warn the smaller ones."

Tierra bobbed her head. "That would work. That's similar to the Bioluminescent Forest's basic protocol, for instances like this." Seeing Alada's confusion, she continued, "Remember when we all planned safety drills for our territories? … At the beginning?"

Alada thought back to when all four Guardians were first together, discussing plans for the individual territories.

"Should we tell them who we are? If you think it's truly that serious, should we step into our Guardian-given power?" Tierra asked.

Alada was watching the elders talk amongst themselves; they were getting thoroughly riled at this point. Still, she shook her head. "No…" she muttered, scanning the burnt buildings again.

A stone wall near the village shrine had scorch marks —

but they weren't random. They curled in a jagged spiral, claw-like. Another building's wooden door was blackened except for a perfectly untouched circle in its center, as if something had shielded it from the fire completely.

"Something doesn't feel right," she said more firmly. "We should remain in our passive cover characters — for now."

Alada could sense Tierra's discontent. Tierra nudged Alada to follow her after hearing Moss discuss burying the fallen and getting the town back into their natural rhythm. "We don't bow to anyone…" It sounded fine and dandy until Alada heard him say, "We should notify the Guardian, Tierra, of this."

Tierra had instinctively turned her head toward the sound of her name; no one noticed.

"How do we tell her?" asked an elder female, Rosemary.

"Send her a message at her shrine?" asked Moss of Rosemary.

"That may be where we're at. Let's try."

Another elder handed Moss a piece of paper, who wrote with a large purple quill.

"How does this sound?" he said after he finished writing his plea. "O, great Guardian of the forest, Gata de la Tierra, we have been attacked by beasts. They left a marking stating we were under the control of The Phantom. Please find it in your grandiose heart to help save us from the tyranny of this Phantom threat. We are your humble, loyal followers. We will support you and your great wisdomous wisdom."

"That sounds pleasant enough," Rosemary stated.

"What makes her think I need lots of praise to come

help?" Tierra scoffed, though a slight flick of her tail betrayed her pique.

Alada raised an eyebrow. "You adored those prizes. And I saw how your claws scratched your winnings when Birch earned the same."

"What does that have to do with anything?"

"You like praise, Tierra," Alada stated flatly.

Tierra hesitated — just a second — then shrugged. "Everyone likes praise."

"But you need it," Alada said gently. "That's not a bad thing. It just means you've been alone too long."

Tierra looked away, pretending to check her claws. "Well... praise reminds me I exist. Makes the quiet less loud, I guess." She brightened, bouncing back into her usual tone. "Anyway, this letter is decent enough. They'll get my help — flattery or not."

Alada didn't engage further. Enough had been said, and the silence conveyed even more.

Together, the elders walked to the shrine located in the center of town. Moss dropped the paper into the enchanted water and it promptly poofed into a small cloud of leaves.

"She has heard us!" they all celebrated. "That was certainly faster than normal. She must have seen what happened."

"I certainly did," Tierra said to Alada with amusement in her eyes. She closed her eyes, concentrating.

"Look! A response already!" cheered Moss. "We are so blessed." Moss and the elders peered into the sacred water and saw words forming beneath the surface:

Aftermath

Safety Protocol One enacted. Reminder:
Remain calm. Do not attract attention to the village.
No fireworks or loud events until the danger has passed.
You will receive notice when all is safe.
Wait in the village unless called into action.
Send messengers to the small villages nearby to warn them.
Tell each village to warn any other smaller villages.

The elders read aloud the message as if chanting to the great and powerful Gata de la Tierra.

"We shall rest assured that the glorious Gata de la Tierra has bestowed her awareness and blessings on us all. We shall tell the village and rejoice in our renewed hope and freedom, uh, quietly," said Moss.

"That'll do," Tierra said, sighing deeply.

"No," Alada stated. "You still need to explain what we know; let them know how dangerous this is, remember?" Her whispers were hardly audible.

Tierra smiled. "Oh, right, yeah." She stood and concentrated once more, and before long, more words formed beneath the surface of the sacred water:

These beasts are not your typical foes.
They can glitch in and out of existence.
Do not engage, should they ever come around again.
Send notice to the other villages if you need more help.

Rest assured, the great Gata de la Tierra is looking into this.

"There," Tierra said, looking over at Alada, who had just read the notice and stood frowning at her. "Okay, fine." Concentrating once more, more words emerged under the surface:

Alada de la Gata is also looking into this.

Tierra peeked at Alada who still didn't look fully satisfied in her facial expressions. Seeing this, she concentrated yet again.

The Guardians are looking into this.

"Satisfied?" Tierra mewed, to which Alada nodded brusquely, turning away.

"And now, time to take our leave," Alada whispered. "We need to go warn the other bigger villages." With remarkably little effort, Alada strode briskly away with Tierra at her heels. As they passed by the boulder with the writing on it, they overheard Grandpa continuing his story. At this point, there were winged rabbits flying around, eating lettuce from the Garden of Greatness. Tierra laughed softly. She noted that most of the Meus were still sitting circled around Grandpa while he rambled on.

Just beyond the villagers' line of sight, Tierra turned to

Alada, ready to suggest tree-travel. Alada's scowl stopped her mid-breath—then a flicker of movement behind Alada's shoulder caught her attention.

"Birch," Tierra said. "May we help you?"

He looked uncomfortable with his hands nervously tapping his own leg. "I wanted to talk with you more about the beasts, but I then remembered you're not from our village. I wanted to catch you before you went home." He approached and stood adjacent to Alada. "Where do you live again? Which village?"

Tierra didn't want to associate herself to any one village … because she couldn't. "I'm pretty nomadic. I love to travel."

"Then you must have seen many places. This is fantastic! I was thinking of warning the other villages. It's the least I can do. Were you going to do that too?" he asked, coming close, though not waiting for a response, "I'd love to join you. When the fire started, I thought I was going to freeze. Not out of fear — I've seen worse. But because I never once saved anyone." He paused. "I lived," he turned to Tierra, "to your point. But it feels that's all I ever do. You both… you didn't even hesitate to jump in and defend others you don't even know. I need to be like that. If we go together, you can teach me and we could travel together. You could make sure we visit them all." Tierra's face fell as he continued. "I only know of a few to the west and one to the east. The majority of my family is … on the way."

Well crap.

"Uhh, well," Tierra began, looking over at Alada with an

expression of *how can we decline a plea like that?* She looked back and forth between Alada and Birch until she finally answered, "Sure, the more the merrier…"

"Thank you so much! This will be great. Just give me a minute to get my things and let everyone know where I'm going." He scampered off.

Tierra sighed. "There goes tree traveling."

"The swiftest path is not always the wisest," Alada said. "After all, we are still in mortal form. We don't know if this is a full invasion of all Felina or a local issue. Keeping our cover still feels like the cautious step. We'll know exactly when to drop the act."

"True."

The sun had sunk low in the sky before Birch had finally returned with a small bag in his paws. "I'm ready. Let's head out. Thanks for waiting, Holly," Birch said. "Where to first? My parents' village? That would be great because it's on the way to Tierra Town. It's a great rest point."

He hadn't waited for a response, but they had to begin somewhere anyway.

"And where might that be?" asked Tierra, leading off down the trail.

"Stone Creek village." His eyes lit up. "That's where I was born."

Tierra and Alada exchanged a look. This journey had just gotten more complicated.

Chapter 7

The Lost Labyrinth

Jasmine," Birch said, wheezing. "Holly! Wait up!" He bent over, panting. As he looked up, both Alada and Tierra were standing over him… completely serene. No sweat. No panting. In fact, they looked perfectly refreshed, with their bright eyes and soft floral scent.

"Need another break?" Tierra asked.

His panting prohibited additional words, so he just nodded and knelt onto the spongy leaf mold. Snatching his own belt bag from behind himself, he clutched the water pouch, and held it over his mouth to drink. Drops dripped lazily out onto his hot tongue. Out again.

Tierra tossed him her completely full and still cool water pouch.

"I can't keep taking all your water," he said, tossing it back … reluctantly.

Tierra hadn't even budged her body or looked at the pouch itself as she caught it. "Well, I don't really get thirsty much when I travel."

He couldn't control his face, which contorted into disbelief. "We've been walking for eight hours and you've only filled your water *once*! Because *I* drank it all the first time!"

"Don't worry, it's only six more hours until we get to Stone Creek," Tierra replied with no sign of fatigue.

Alada eyed him as she set her things onto a fallen log. "You're right. Maybe now is a good time to rest. We've been walking all night after all. And besides, we all did just have quite a battle and no time to rest. How does that sound, Holly, a little break?"

Tierra hesistated, clearly ready to keep trecking. "Well, okay, sure. That's fine. I'll get some food up for us all," Tierra replied as she padded off into the forest, leaving them alone.

"She always seems to have infinite energy, and you too. How do you do it? Sugar, coffee, herbs, mushrooms?" Birch asked. He needed to know what helped them walk for so long, if he ever wanted to keep up.

Alada thought for a moment, settling herself onto a moss-covered mound of dirt. It was cool to the touch, somewhat squishy, and very refreshing. "Just a gift, I suppose."

His face fell.

Tierra soon strolled towards them with her paws full of colorful fruits and berries, which were already semi-squished and dripping glowing pink juice into her fur.

"Birch, did you bring any popple cream or sweet sap? If you didn't, I have cold-pressed Honey Elixir we could use instead."

"But wait, what is all this for? What are you making?" he asked, still hardly able to stand.

Tierra looked at her armfuls of assorted delicacies. "My famous Tierra de la Gata power smoothie. It's ultra-heathy and it should help you get back on your feet again."

Eyes large and full of bewilderment, he soon nodded his head and rummaged through his small sack. "I have popple milk you can use or some crystal lilac for an energy boost..." He handed her the jar once her hands were free of the sweets, which now lay on a flat rock.

"Thank you," Tierra said as she produced a curiously tall bowl, almost vase-like, crafted from dark, polished wood. The rim was inlaid with pressed leaves — some still fragrant — while vines had been carefully trained and dried into a firm spiral along the side. These vines supported a crank arm made from bent willow and twine-wrapped joints, and a small stone weight dangled beneath, acting as a counter-balance.

Inside, two flat wooden paddles crossed like windmill blades, connected by a central stem that turned when the crank was spun. "I call it a hand-blender," Tierra announced proudly, settling it into a carved stump to brace it. "Manual, vine-crank powered, mess-free — mostly." She tipped in the whole jar of popple milk, followed it with the other foraged ingredients, and then swiftly turned the crank, pulverizing it all into a pink-swirled, creamy delight.

"Where did she get that?" Birch wondered, eyeing the contraption warily as the paddles began to spin with a surprisingly smooth rhythm. "The Central Village still uses grinding rocks and blending bowls," he said aloud, stepping closer.

"I love how the Central Village honors the foundational, natural ways," Tierra replied warmly. "But I wanted to blend—" she flashed a grin, "pun intended—some of the convenience I've seen in other villages with our timeless earth-based traditions."

She carefully poured the drink from the bowl's spout into carved wooden cups, a thin line of froth forming along the edge. "Using what the land gives us, as it desires," she added.

"I wouldn't mind an upgrade," Birch admitted, taking a cup and sniffing its contents appreciatively.

"I've seen versions of this that use electricity in the Nya homeland," Alada said softly, her voice trailing at the end. *Should I have said that?*

Birch didn't seem to notice. "I've passed through a village or two with electricity. Pretty impressive," he admitted. "Still… I've got a soft spot for the old ways. Guess I'm just stuck in my preferences."

"This wild suckleberry hits the sweet spot," Alada remarked, sipping slowly. "It's fall in a drink."

"The dew-lillies are my absolute favorite in winter," Tierra noted. "Fall? I'd say butterberries from the southern peaks. Haven't had them in ages," she added, now silent as she drank.

"Suckleberries are my absolute favorite sweet from these parts," Alada crooned. "The sweetness mixed with the hint of fire and semi-tang on the back of the tongue... divine." She let her head fall back as she savored the flavor. "My second favorite is the twisted sugar bean vine from Coral's territory."

"Whose Coral?" Birch asked, practically licking the foam from his cup.

Alada suddenly found herself holding her breath. Her cup hovered near her lips, forgotten. "Oh, I meant the Goddess Coralees has such a lovely area by the ocean. I probably shouldn't have been so informal. I'm sorry if that was offensive."

"No, that's okay. Each Guardian is different and you two clearly have been around, so it would make sense you might be less connected to one specific Guardian and more open to informal acceptance of them all," he said, now looking at the bird-like lunar moths nearby with a focused interest.

"Those sugar beans you mentioned are more north," Tierra remarked, sipping her smoothy. "So," she continued, leaning an arm on a nearby stump, "We'll be to Stone Creek by the afternoon or evening." She looked around in all directions. "If we head east, we'll carve off two hours of travel."

Birch knew this direction and couldn't believe anyone in their right mind would suggest such a shortcut. "That's straight through the Lost Labyrinth." He stared, unblinking, at Tierra.

Alada's eyes widened at his response and turned her attention to Tierra as well. "Is there something wrong with the

Lost Labyrinth? I don't recall there being an issue, but has one come up?"

Tierra shrugged. "Nothing, it's just the most stupefying maze I am the champion of." Her matter-of-fact tone practically echoed in her self-proclamation.

Disbelieving his own ears, which was a first as he prided himself on his hearing and his ability to listen (just as the elders had taught him), he struggled to come up with a response to such an arrogant, impossible claim. "Champion?" He shook his head. "It is well-known — not even a legend — that anyone who enters does not come out. Even the best of the best seekers have gone in and not made it out … on their own at least."

She looked away, now licking what juice she could out of her blender and using her water to clean it.

Alada promptly looked at her, half-amusedly glaring.

"Well, I can find my way around in there like the back of my head — which has fur." Tierra nodded, satisfied with her perception of an analogy.

"I know you say you're a champion of the Lost Labyrinth," he said, "But I've never heard of such a thing. Only, Tierra, the great, glorious, majestic–"

"Gorgeous?" Tierra whispered, still licking her paws.

"Heavenly, divine, and super-humble–"

Alada spit the water she was drinking all over him. She snorted loudly and couldn't get a grip as laughter consumed her.

He stopped, and a spark of anger formed in his stomach. "What? Do you not believe in her?"

Alada hastily gained composure as she caught his eye. "Oh, no … no, I do! I just am not sure that description fits her so accurately."

"Of course it does. The great goddess wrote it herself on the Divine Scroll of Tierra!"

Alada's wide-eyed stare borderlined another bout of hysterics. "She wrote it herself, eh? Sorry, I guess I'm not familiar with the scroll."

"I agree with his statement. She is proud of her humbleness indeed," Tierra said, bowing her head in respect of the wondrous goddess.

Alada shook her head, unimpressed.

None of them got back up. Even Tierra and Alada suddenly felt a desire to sleep. Beyond tired, none of them had even noticed that they had lazily drifted to sleep on what was supposed to be a break.

As morning dawned, Tierra was still trying to convince Birch that the Lost Labyrinth was the fastest way to go. Having not slept well despite falling asleep fast, Birch found himself more easily irritable while trying to convince *Holly* that wanting to go that way was a guaranteed death wish. All the while, Alada did not have a preference.

"Is there a compromise that you both can make?" Alada suggested.

"No," he and Tierra said at once.

Tierra continued, "The Lost Labyrinth is perfectly fine, I

assure you … aside from the Wishes."

"The *what?*" Birch said. He shook his head. *There is no changing her opinion.* He raised his paws up in defeat and said with a sigh, "Fine, you win. We can go through the Lost Labrinth."

"Great! It is just this way," Holly said as she padded off to where must be east. "The only thing we have to do is stick together and you'll be fine."

Wishes … now why does that sound familiar? Birch thought.

Chapter 8
The Voices

Holly led them down a long and winding trail, which appeared completely abandoned with its overgrown assortment of bushes and vines.

Maybe this won't be so bad. I do recall one of the elders telling a story of Tierra saving lost Meus from here. He figured that if worse came to worse — Hey! At least he'd get to meet a Guardian. He hastily wound himself through the undergrowth, not wanting to lose sight of his companions.

"Well, come on, the Lost Labrinth is just this way!" Tierra said. "Oh, and watch your step, Jazzy."

"Don't call me that … Holl."

"Hey, and try not to lag in the back too much!" Tierra called back to Birch as she glanced over her shoulder.

Why call me out for lagging now? I've been in the back this whole time. Maybe she thinks I'm slow. I'll show her I'm not, Birch thought. *Maybe I've been slowing them down too much. And to think that I was one of the strongest Meus in the village … No, I still am. I just can't doubt myself.* He picked up his pace and jogged ahead of Holly and Jasmine, ignoring the ache of his tired legs.

"Er, Birch, what's up?" Alada asked, her tone slightly cautious.

"What's up? The canopy, duh," Tierra quipped, chuckling at her own joke.

"Amusing as always, but—"

Birch suddenly picked up his pace even more. He didn't want to hear any explanations or reasons or excuses made for him.

"Wait, Birch!" Alada called after him, but he was already too far ahead — and off the path.

Branches brushed his arms as he charged through the undergrowth, no longer hearing their voices behind him. The glowing forest dimmed around him, the trail dissolving into thickets and shadow.

"Holly?" he said uncertainly. "Jasmine?"

His eyes widened; he saw movement in a patch of large ferns. Shifting his paws, he bolted off toward the rustling, hoping to find his friends. *For a glowing forest, it sure is getting hard to see.*

He reached the ferns and pushed them aside. Stepping forward, his paw caught on a well-hidden python vine. It swiftly wrapped itself around Birch's waist. "Aaahh!" *What the? I've never had to deal with one of these before... Well, I guess except that one time when I found one sprouting near my house once. What did I do that time? ...* "Uh...? Help! Hooolly? Jaaazmine?! How do I get out?"

"You just have to suffocate it back," came a somewhat

familiar voice. Only somewhat, though.

"Who said that? Holly, is that you?"

"Sure, this is Holly. I can be a Holly."

Birch squinted into the shadows. That didn't sound right. "I just have to *suffocate* it, you say? … How?"

"By dancing backward."

"Oh, so—" The vine suddenly tightened around his throat. Birch panicked and immediately launched into a bizarre hula: waving his paws, wiggling his hips, and flailing his tail as if on fire.

Please let this work, he thought, eyes bulging.

"Ha, ha, ha!" the voice giggled.

Though his awful dancing didn't appear to weaken it, he could wriggle out of the vine's grasp. Fatigued yet again, he started searching.

A loud, sharp *snap* echoed behind him.

Startled, he spun around. "Holly, come out!"

Something brushed the tips of his ears. His heart pounded in his chest. He heard himself faintly wheezing. The world around him spun slightly. He focused on his ears — willing himself to be able to hear someone trying to rescue him.

Silence…

Looking up, he saw a tightly woven canopy high above him.

"That could never touch me … or maybe it could?"

"Is Holly sure it absolutely could not? Ha, ha, ha — Tierra's so funny," came a voice again.

"Tierra?! Is that you? Oh, please help me, great goddess.

Can you tell me where to go?"

"Right, down, under."

"Under me?" He started clawing franticly at the hard soil.

"Now, now, not left up over. Just run in the north direction. Then leap south twice."

Sitting up, he looked around.

North … right. I need to get back. I need to find Holly.

Not knowing where north was, he just picked a direction and went with it. He ran twenty yards, then leapt back twice and found himself in the spot he began.

"Ha, ha. So silly, so silly…"

"I'm not *silly* … am I…?" He clutched the long tuffs of fur behind his ears in frustration. *She's not right. She's not right,* Birch thought. *She's wrong. Everything is wrong. Why?*

"Why not? Ha, ha, ha!"

"Don't yer lose hope now, boy. You's gotta long way to go. Besides, sonny, that ain't even the *real* Gata de la Tierra yer been talkin' to," a male elderly voice said suddenly.

"Don't listen to *him.* He doesn't know what he's saying!" the shrill voice of Tierra exclaimed with rage.

He felt a strong paw on his shoulder, though no one was there.

"You've heard her. Ya know her. Don't pay attention to the voices that sound like ya loved ones, now good luck. Ya still got a way to go, sonny," the male said.

"Why would I not listen to Tierra? She helps everyone out of here!" Birch argued.

The old male voice chuckled. "Yes, and no. The real Tierra helps. The fake Tierras will get you more lost."

Birch could hardly believe his own ears. "How can you tell the difference!?" he all but screamed.

"I am the real Tierra!" came the shrill call of the voice he had been hearing already. "How dare you doubt me!"

"But, I…"

"Did that voice of this Tierra help you?" the male voice asked.

"Well, I thought so…" Birch looked all around to see if he could spot a location of the voices.

"Of course I helped him!" the Tierra-voice called again. "Don't listen to that old grumple."

"But—I don't know where to go! Please, can you help me?" Birch pleaded, his paws clutched together.

"Oh, but you *DO* know where to go, sonny," the male said.

I may as well just trust myself to find my way out. Can't get much worse, I'm already lost anyway.

He bolted off at a run down a long corridor-like aisle lined with thick bramble, branches, and stone.

"Birch? Birch! Where are you?" came a familiar voice.

He stopped midway down the corridor when an alternative path opened directly *through* the large boulder. Distracted by the melting rock, he stared as the new direction appeared. When he looked back toward his original heading, that path had mysteriously closed off as if it had never been there. *Guess I'll go this way,* he thought. *No wonder everyone goes missing in here.*

"Greetings, Meu. You have entered the Lost Labyrinth." This voice sounded angelic and echoed slightly all around him.

You must be Tierra, he thought. *The real Tierra.*

"What is it you wish most?" asked the voice. *"Wish with all your heart for what you desire most right now."*

I wish I could get out of this maze right now, he prayed.

Immediately, a new and welcoming path appeared, and at the end was a bright, shining light. He ran toward it and his lungs tighten with fatigue as he neared the end of the long aisle. *Thank you, Tierra! Thank you, Tierra!* he thought repeatedly.

As he neared it, the source of the light revealed itself — a large, golden trophy surrounded by four other passageways. He approached the trophy slowly and saw an inscription: *Keep Wishing Harder.*

I wish someone would tell me how to get out of here! he thought, bitterly. He struck at the trophy with his paw, but his paw merely went through it as if it were an illusion.

"Yaaaaaa!" he hissed and roared.

"You can get out through the second aisle," the angelic voice called.

He wasn't sure if she meant the second from the left or right. He raced down the one on the right because, well — did it really matter at this point?

"I want to be back with Holly and Jasmine," he pouted, continuing to mutter to himself. "Tierra saved everyone I know … maybe she didn't save some. Maybe not everyone makes it out. Only those who live to tell the stories."

Suddenly, a ghost-like figure with torn traveling robes, burst from the brush and barreled right for him, screaming all the while. Birch jumped and fell backward, nearly skewering himself on a jagged branch.

The figure stopped abruptly, laughing so hysterically that it painlessly fell into a thicket of thorny brambles. "Everyone usually makes it out of here alive, but you may be the first one who doesn't!" it teased heartlessly. "Keep wishing!"

As Birch got up, he saw that a dead end had formed. His path was gone.

"Maybe wish for a way out?" the ghost laughed.

"Who are you?" Birch asked.

The ghost floated beside him in a menacing way until he heard the question — to which he stopped and appeared to come out of whatever evil personality he had been portraying. The ghost merely stared.

"So, either you forgot, or you don't know, or you don't want to tell me," Birch added.

The ghost's outfit also appeared to change, from ragged, torn robes into a neatly composed and traditional Meu outfit.

"Uh, do you realize your outfit has changed?" Birch asked.

The ghost opened his mouth, but no words came out.

"You look familiar," Birch stated as he walked back toward where the trophy had been, which had disappeared. "Yeah, you look like an elder from our village. He had gotten lost in the maze when he was young. You look like a younger version of him."

Birch began walking away, he couldn't waste time talking in one place.

The ghost followed him. "How dare you call me a ghost," the ghost claimed.

Birch didn't stop walking to talk. "I didn't call you a ghost. You called yourself one."

"I just want you to know that I'm still alive and young."

"Um, are you sure? How long do you think you've been in here?"

"Not too long. Though I'm trying to get out of here." The ghost's voice lowered further, mumbling, "This was my greatest wish."

Birch stopped to stare at him … he, a ghost, who could clearly fly anywhere in this realm or another… "Well, since you could just fly, why not just fly yourself right out of here?"

Affronted, the male ghost floated up so close to Birch that their noses would have touched … if he had a phsyical one too. "You don't understand where you are. This is not just a maze. Why do you think it takes a goddess to help you escape and not a mere mortal Meu?"

Birch didn't budge nor flinch. "You're the elder, *Moss*."

The ghost's eyes bulged, unblinking. Silent.

"I remember you."

It felt like days. Who truly knew how long it had been?

Voices swirled around him, spouting out nonsense:

"Do you want some water, sir?"

"How about directions?"

"Why don't you try thinking backward and see where that takes you?"

Birch assumed the voices belonged to other ghosts like Moss, though not keen to reveal themselves.

"CHEESE, come get your CHEESE. Right over by the glowing trees."

"Don't think positive, think as negative as you can! Helps with even the most happy-go-lucky situations and getting out of here without her help."

"Why can't she help him? I thought they were friends?"

"She's trying. He's just not listening."

"Do you think our talking helps?"

"No, not at all."

"Oh right! I remember now. Thank you."

"You're welcome!"

Birch walked around for what felt like hours (and it probably was) with no sign of Holly, nor Jasmine, nor freedom. His head ached and his ears pounded. "Oh, looky at this stick. Maybe it will help me FORGET ALL THIS NOISE!!!" he screeched, picking up a thick stick and hitting himself with it — *crack!*

"Yup. Definitely *not* helping." He threw the stick back down to the ground. "Oh, sound of O, can you tell me, do you know? Where I need to go…" he sang, not even paying attention to where he was going anymore.

Chapter 8

Tired. O, so tired. Must sleep, he thought.

"I'm just going to rest for a moment. We've been in here all day."

"Why try to sleep if life is already a dream?!" Moss doubled over, laughing. He had a knack for revealing himself only for entertaining commentary.

Ignoring the ghost, Birch murmured to himself before falling asleep, "Maybe I'll have better luck wishing tomorrow."

The last thing he remembered before passing out was a set of eyes looking at him from behind a tree. *Tierra? Nah, I doubt it.*

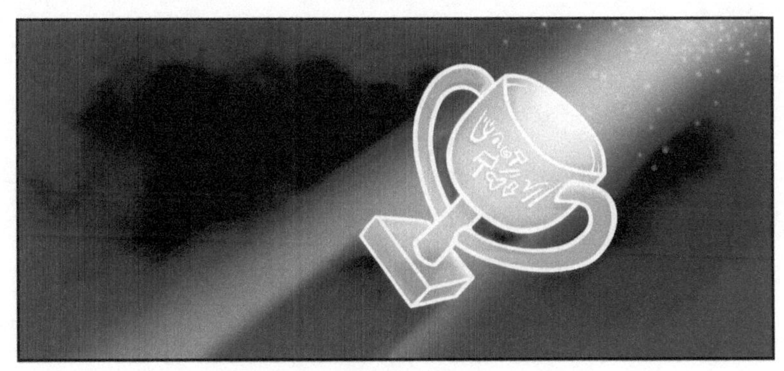

Chapter 9

Nightmare

Holly? Jasmine? Am I still in the village? He sat up, rubbing his eyes. He blinked into the suffocating dark. The ground beneath him felt too smooth, too still — like polished stone, or nothing at all. A faint light above him caught his eye.

Growing closer, he realized the light was actually a small glowing object falling in slow-motion. Leaping up like he would in zero-gravity, he caught it and noticed it was a small version of the Wish Harder trophy.

"What?" his voice echoed endlessly around him, slowly fading into silence.

Even though it was pitch-black, he could still see his reflection in the golden trophy. His fur looked messy, his eyes were tired and desperate, and he had torn the tip of his ear.

"Is that *me?*"

He touched his reflection. The golden surface warped, but the haunted eyes staring back didn't.

He looked harder, and his reflection changed. Suddenly,

a vision of his mother emerged from the golden reflection. Her face contorted in terror, her eyes fixated on something unknown — she was yelling something. The vision faded, leaving the echo of his mother's screams ringing and ringing and ringing in his ears. He could feel his heart pounding in his chest and as he breathed in, he nearly choked on his own saliva. His raised hackles felt uncomfortable under his clothes.

"Wish harder" again appeared on the trophy, and again fading away, this time he saw once again his own reflection. Only his own breathing was audible alongside his heartbeat. Speechless. Powerless. Thoughtless. Time stood still. His mother's scream echoed on a loop until even memory gave way — it wasn't a play anymore. It was real.

"So–"

Birch screamed and hissed as he jumped away from the voice. Then he saw Moss, standing unamused.

"You forgot I was here, didn't you?" Moss asked.

Birch only breathed deeply, trying to catch his breath.

"Wish harder, huh?" Moss asked. "It hasn't worked yet, but you have to keep at it."

Birch continued to calm his breathing.

"Well…? Aren't you going to say something? Something like, 'Oh, Moss. Why didn't I think of that before? You're so wise.'"

Birch stared, unamused.

"'You're amazing. You should be the next god of the Lost Labyrinth,'" Moss added with a flourish.

Birch's face didn't move. The silence hung heavy — just long enough to stop the act cold.

"What do you wish for most?" Birch asked flatly.

Moss chuckled. "To get out of here, of course."

Birch shook his head. "No, that's not your greatest wish. *Who* are you wanting to get out of here *for?*"

Moss' eyes bulged, and moments later, his mouth drooped. There was no dance, no rendition of his exceptional abilities or handsome features, nor any sign of levity or flippant attitudes.

"Well?" asked Birch. "You seemed so keen on talking … cat catch your tongue?" He smirked to himself. *Clever.*

But Moss didn't answer. He just stood there completely stunned into either silence or memory. But as the silence continued to prevail and Moss continued to stand there staring at him, then at the ground, it occurred to Birch that maybe it wasn't a memory. Maybe … Moss had forgotten.

"Moss?"

Moss refused to look at him, and then his image flickered between the current aged Moss he knew from the village and his ghostly appearance.

"Moss?"

Still, Moss could barely make eye contact.

"… You don't remember…" Birch whispered. "You only know you're wishing to leave."

Moss didn't move nor answer. He simply vanished.

Birch understood. He himself didn't know how long he'd been here, how the Labyrinth became full of ghosts and otherworldly magic and beings, nor how or if he would leave … he, too, wanted to vanish in that moment. He almost wished it. Instead, he noticed a small fire that had appeared, burning softly behind him and sat beside it.

The flames didn't offer warmth — only a flickering glow, as if the fire itself wasn't sure it was real. Birch curled around it anyway, afraid to sleep, afraid to forget why he was even trying to find a way out.

Chapter 10

Gnarla

Moss didn't appear all day.

Birch had continued walking around the Labyrinth, now used to being lost. *Being lost is being found*, he thought. *Lost is all there is.* He walked down a narrow walkway only to be cut off by a bush that instantly grew before him. Without thinking, he merely backed up as if this was a normal, everyday occurrence.

"Wish I could warn my mother. Wish I could warn my mother," he muttered under his breath as he ventured an alternative path, looking down at the ground as he meandered around. *I wish Tierra would rescue me like she did everyone else. I wish any of the gods would rescue me. I wish Holly hadn't sucked me into this cursed place.* Suddenly, he walked straight into a tree, face-first, as if the forest itself had decided to interrupt his pity party.

"Whoooooo arrrree yooouuuu to bummmp meeee?" the tree demanded in response to his carelessness.

"No one," Birch answered. "Sorry." He stepped over a root to leave, but the tree lifted the root higher and tripped him.

"Nooooooooot sooo fassssst," demanded the tree. "Wheeerrreee arrreee youuu goooinnngg sooo fasssst? Theeeerreee's nooowheeerrree to gooo."

"Out of here."

The tree slowly laughed … at him.

Birch glared up into the tree's eyes, which had slowly opened near its first branch.

"Who are you?" Birch asked.

The tree took a long, slow drawling breath. "Nooot thaaat iiit matteeerrrs…"

"That's quite a name," Birch muttered. "Want me to come back when you've finished saying it?"

The tree stared at him, amused at least. "Myyyyyy naaaaammee iiiiissss Gnarllla thhhheeee…"

"So, Grumpy Tree?" Birch offered. "Rude Tree? You pick."

Gnarla lifted a large root and tripped him again from behind. Again, she laughed … at him.

"Do you know how to get out of here?" Birch asked, not expecting an answer of any value, but enjoying having someone to talk to since he sensed she meant no harm.

"Nooot thaaaat it maaatteeerrrs … but yes."

"And how would you do that?" he asked.

A low-rumbled throat laugh emerged from the ancient, bitter tree. "Byyyy leeeaaaavvviiinnngggg."

"Is there a tactic you'd recommend on *how* to leave?"

"Byyy waaaalkiiinnng … Yoouu aaareee slllooooww fooor sssooommmeeeooonnne wiiith twoooo leeegs."

"And you're not helpful," Birch remarked.

Gnarla raised an eyebrow and let out a long, dreadful sigh. "Mooore heeelpfuul than yoouuu knooow."

"If walking is your best advice to getting out of here…"

Gnarla sat with her eyes closed.

"Do you actually have any other useful information?"

Gnarla let out a long, dreadful sigh … again. "Not that iiit maaatteeeerrrs.… but yes." She opened her eyes, peering this way and that. Softly, she whispered, "Dooonnn't wwwiiiiiisssh. Dooonnnn't liiiissssteeenn toooo…" Gnarla, who spoke slowly, suddenly screeched in agony as Birch jumped back just barely missing the burst of flames that had come out of nowhere.

A vision or a figure or a ghost vanished from behind the fire blaze with a most pleased, malicious grin on her face. She looked like … *but it couldn't be.* The wails and moans of Gnarla's burning limbs shook Birch from his reverie. He glanced around for a means to douse the blue-orange flames.

A murky, stagnant pond festered nearby, but with nothing to carry water in, Birch needed another idea. Think. He dropped to his knees, scooped up handfuls of dirt, and hurled them into the flames, hoping to smother the fire. Ash and smoke billowed back at him, but he kept going — more dirt, more flinging. It wasn't much, but it was all he had.

Gnarla now began coughing from the dirt being flung into her mouth and eyes … amidst her cries of agony. "Myyy eyes! Myyy boooodyyy!"

Okay, now what? thought Birch while frantically looking for a way to gather more water than his two paws could hold. Amidst the fire's crackles and Gnarla's painful moans and wails, he tried to get his mind to think. *Think!* He searched around. *Think!*

"Hurry! Hurry!" cried Moss, suddenly appearing and carrying a pail of water as ghostly as he was. Birch watched as Moss threw the water on Gnarla.

How could ghost-water help her? he thought, desperately.

But it did help. The blue flame was ebbing and fading away with each pail Moss through on her. "Hurry! Grab a pail!" commanded Moss again. "Hurry!"

Birch looked around and did indeed spot an old, rusted pail by the murky pond. He lunged for it, ripping it free from the weeds and other plants that were strangling it to the ground. He shoved it into the cool water and pulled it up with substantial force. Water seeped quickly out of the rusted holes, so he lumbered faster despite the off-balance weight to one side. Using both paws to hold the pail, he threw the water onto Gnarla, who seemed to cry louder at this relief.

He ran and carried the pail back and forth from Gnarla to the stale pond. *I'm coming, Gnarla! I'm coming! I'm coming!* he thought. He could no longer tell if he was talking or thinking, and he kept moving as quickly as his feet would carry him. His arms felt numb as he carried bucket after bucket to and from the pond as the flames continued engulfing Gnarla.

After some time, though, the fire smoldered, and Gnarla's trunk and branches went out. Breathless, he dropped to the ground and let the pail clatter down beside him. He sat staring at Gnarla, whose eyes were closed. Her face blended so well with the bark that he wouldn't have known a face even existed if she hadn't spoken to him before.

Her thick branches were now brittle and charred. Pain clearly radiated from every limb.

Moss, for once, was silent, looking at his pail as if it were suddenly very fascinating.

Birch felt like passing out. He could barely lift his arms, let alone keep his body upright much longer. Yet he noticed among Gnarla's fresh burns were other older, darker spots amongst her trunk and branches. Some branches had broken off, charred, but not from this fire. Burn marks dotted her all over; some marks flanked her entire left side.

Gnarla's eyes drooped open as she stared blankly at the ground before her. Birch sensed a prison-like feeling — to be rooted in one spot and burned repeatedly … stuck in a place like this … His heart sank. "Has this happened before? Or were those other marks an accident?"

Gnarla didn't look up, nor did she make her drawn out, annoyed-with-Meus exhale Birch had come to expect.

Among the silence, Birch found his answer. He touched the brittle sap at the base of her trunk — it flaked off like burnt sugar. Not new. Not from today. "Not an accident," he mumbled softly.

Gnarla stared at the ground. A spot she always saw. A tear of sap welled up in her eyes, but she did not cry. She closed her eyes as if giving herself a private moment. In fact, it was the only privacy she could ever have.

And for a long time, he simply sat beside her. Just being. It was all he could offer.

Much later, as the silence settled into something softer, Birch stirred where he sat on the bare ground. The irritation he once felt toward her had long faded. Now, he only wanted connection.

"Please," Birch asked. "Why were you burned? That cat, the one in the flames … she looked … very familiar. Why did she hurt you?"

He heard a low inhale as Gnarla opened her eyes, still peering at the ground.

"She looked … like a cat I've been traveling with. But she can't be here. Was that being just another ghost? Someone trying to trick me?" he asked. Gnarla didn't speak, which left an uncomfortable silence to fill. "Seems like everyone and everything is trying to trick me in here, so that I always stay here forever. Just like Moss." He sat down with his chin to his knees. "This place makes no sense," he whispered. He let tears flow down his face and soak into his pant legs as sap quietly flowed from Gnarla's eyes.

He let the tears continue to flow, now observing Gnarla's burns about her trunk and limbs. An old pile of sap sat at the bottom of her trunk in a hardened pile — old sap upon hardened ancient sap.

He sat up at this revelation, wiping the tears from his eyes. "You *were* telling the truth." He stood up — renewed by the energy of truth. "You *were* telling the truth." He stepped toward her, inspecting the marks closely. "These are punishments for telling the truth!" When he turned his gaze to her face, Gnarla locked eyes with his, yet she said nothing. "You're probably the only sane being here!"

For once, Gnarla appeared almost youthful with her eyebrows up and eyes full of light.

"Why would anyone want to punish you for telling the truth?" he asked, but Gnarla didn't reply. He sighed. "You can't tell me without getting punished again, huh? I bet you were telling me how to actually get out of here."

"Birch! Biiirrrch!" he heard in the near-ish distance. It sounded just like Holly.

"I'm hearing voices again," he told Gnarla. "Guess it's pretty common here." Still, he felt he had at least found a lifeboat of sanity. She was grumpy and may be bitter at life, but at least Gnarla had an innate direction with how this labyrinth truly worked.

"Youuu muuussst fooolllooowww thaaat voiiiiccceee," Gnarla said. "Gooo nooowww."

"No," Birch said. "Those are just ghosts and other demented beings trying to confuse me. This place makes you not trust anyone…. Even if they *are* telling the truth." He lowered his head and shifted his weight from one foot to another. "I'm sorry, Gnarla, for how I treated you. I wish I could help you." Seeing her rooted in one spot, so clearly ancient, was cause for tears to well up in his eyes. There was no way to help her. This is where she lives.

This one … single … spot.

For as long as she lived.

Again, the voice of Holly called out, "Birch! Where are you? I spy with my little eye … something green."

"Everything is green!" a voice like Jasmine's responded.

The voices started to fade.

"Truuussst meee nooowww." Gnarla's wide eyes and tone brought Birch to the truth of the present moment. "Saaavvveee meee byyy truuussstinnngg meee nooowww. Yooouuurrr giffft of feeet willl saaavvveee yooouuu."

"But I want to help us both."

"I am meaaannnt toooo beee heeerrreee. Thiiisss iiisss okaaayy. Yooouuu haaavveee giivveeen meee the greaaateeessst giiiffft of beeellliiieeevvvinng annnd lisssteeeninng toooo meee."

Birch realized he needed to trust her and go, and he etched her woody old smile into his memory.

"Nooowww gooo. Quiiickk!"

Birch nodded, smiled, and took off running toward the fading voices of what he desperately hoped were the real Holly and Jasmine. And then—there they were! Just ahead!

But in true labyrinth fashion, a massive, tangled bush erupted from the ground between them, cutting off his view.

Of course. Birch skidded to a halt. *I wouldn't expect anything less from this accursed place.* "Holly! Jasmine! I'm behind the bush! Help me!" he cried.

No answer.

"Don't wish," he told himself.

In a flash, Tierra stood beside him, having vaulted over the top.

"I'll just wait here," Jasmine said from the other side.

Holly... she looked so similar to the face he had seen in the flames. Could she have hurt Gnarla? Even though she stood before him, he wasn't entirely sure it was actually her. He had seen and heard her likeness many times already.

She stared at him — apparently unsure she had found the actual Birch.

"Is it really you?" he asked.

She stared at him. "Only one way to find out. Only the real me can lead you out of here. The false impressions of me will lead you nowhere."

He nodded. "Guess there's no harm in following you."

"But there is harm in not." She continued to eye him. "You don't seem too crazy yet. Usually, by now, the Meus I save are holding their knees, talking to themselves, and think I am a birthday cake. Once someone thought I was a ghost. Another thought I was a demon."

"Did you hurt Gnarla?" he asked. He had to know.

Her face contorted. "I would never hurt anyone in here or anywhere, really." She paused. "I guess I do hurt others, like the beasts, if they want to hurt others. So, I suppose it's fair to say that I protect the innocent, and I will hurt those with ill intent toward the them."

Despite attempting to utilize his truth-sayer-lie-detector abilities, he couldn't detect any signs of dishonesty. He didn't answer. He wasn't one hundred percent sure about anything right now.

"How long have I been away — a week? A month?"

"Maybe, I don't know, ten … twelve minutes? Twenty at most."

"… Minutes …"

"Sorry it wasn't sooner. I was busy talking with Jaz!" Tierra said, looking over the shrubbery that divided them and Alada.

*Minutes … **minutes**. Does the word **minute** mean **week** in some other obscure language? Ara-Meuish perhaps? No, that can't be. That language went out the window in the Fallen Era… Meuzu, Aranya, and Frantic paw signals were stopped by the Peace Treaty. Now we all just speak Meuzna, dropping any remains of the Ara language altogether! Fascinating, wouldn't ya think…. Wait, then how would a young Meu know an ancient dialect that is not even known to any of the eldest historians? Is she some sort of time-traveler from another planet!? A-a-a Meu from the Divided Years, that was resurrected and taught how to live in modern time!? If that's what happened to Holly, then what could Jasmine possibly be?*

"Biiirch? Yo 'kay? Come on, Birch, it's about time you had some proper sleep … and maybe a good ol' bath too."

"Aren't you curious about what happened to me in here?"

"I'm well versed in what it does to the minds of those who get lost in here. But if talking about it helps you feel better, go ahead. I'm just glad you didn't go crazy. That's the important thing."

"Yeah..." Birch's mind had wandered off at that point, his eyes directed at the canopy and his steps slowing. *If I'm leaving, then what about Moss? Maybe I can help him get out, too?*

"Birch! If you can't focus, then we can't get you out!"

"Just give me one sec." He needed to find Moss and try to help him out, even if he was just a ghost. Birch ran back to where he last saw Moss with his pail of stale pond water.

Not here ... Uh, maybe here... no.

Pawsteps sounded from behind him, chorused by loud panting. "Birch, what has gotten in to you? We just found you, and now you're running away? Do you need help with something?" Tierra asked in an unpleased stop-with-your-games-now tone. "It's time to go."

"Moss. I need to find him first. At least to say goodbye."

"Moss?" she asked. She shook her head, muttering to herself, "Ur, maybe you're crazier than I thought." She sighed. "Birch, Moss isn't here. He's back at the village, safe and sound."

"Yes, I know that," he snapped. "I'm talking about his ghost!" He stooped over and searched a puddle of muck. His back felt sore, as if Moss had been sitting there the whole time. Swiftly turning his head over his shoulder, he checked just to be sure Moss wasn't actually sitting on his back.

I wish he'd appear already! He fell hard onto his knees in defeat. *Why can't anything in this stupid forest go my way?* With paws trembling in frustration, despair, and hopelessness, he wondered under his breath, *Why wish if you have no hope? Keep wishing, everyone said. But why wish for freedom if you can't help those who sacrificed their wellbeing for yours? Who guided you without help in return? What do you do then? Live with the dissatisfaction that you left someone in the forest after all they have done for you…?*

A soft paw grabbed him, hauling him to his feet. Tierra looked into his eyes with a newfound sense of sympathy. She pulled one of the many twigs from his pelt and said, "If we don't leave now, we won't have enough time to get to your mother's house before supper."

Supper? Really.

"We wouldn't want to leave you here and tell her you got lost because you didn't follow your guide, would we?" She continued brushing more twigs and leaves from his soft striped, cream and orange colored coat as she guided him in the right direction.

"Lost and forced to eat garbage and waste. Oh, the tragedy! Never to be seen again. Fed to the beasts! Sacrificed to the gods!" Tierra's voice grew louder and more exaggerated as she went on telling of all the things that would happen to him. Birch interrupted when Tierra got to where he had dishonored his family name, his nonexistent cow, and how he would be forever cursed — even in the afterlife.

"Holly, if I leave now, can you promise not to tell anyone

that I got lost? And to not punish me by any of your various forms of torture? I strongly prefer not to be sacrificed to anyone."

"Huh?" Tierra said, slightly confused that he would interrupt her in the middle of a monologue that had twisted into a full-on Shakespearian performance with costumes of mud and props made of mushrooms. "Oh yeaaah, we can do that, no torturing or sacrificing, got it," she said, dropping her mighty (stick) sword. She grabbed his paw again and ran off toward the bush she had previously leapt over, and somehow, leapt over it again with Birch in tow.

"Aaaah!" Alada screeched as they both landed on her in a way you'd expect two Meus to land on someone: loudly, with lots of pain and hissing.

"Get — off — of — me — now!" Alada hissed.

"But we just got here!" Tierra said, trying to unmix herself.

"Aaah, ouch! Jeez, what was that for!?"

"Sawee," Tierra apologized through a mouthful of fur.

"*MERT, NERWY,*" Alada struggled to say more than that, her thrashing slowing to a halt.

Birch managed to succeed lifting Tierra onto her feet along with her stylish new backpack called Alada.

Good news: Alada had not passed out. Bad news: She looked like she would happily leave them both in the Lost Labyrinth forever.

"Now, what do you do *before* you leap?" Alada recited for

the fifth time.

"Look," he and Tierra said at once, nonplused.

Having sat down on a log to clean everyone else's fur from between their nails, Tierra and Birch had inadvertently become Alada's captive audience. *I never knew how much Jasmine liked lectures until now*, Birch thought, tiring of the safety drill.

Alada sighed. "Birch, even though you *just* got out of the Labyrinths' magical grasp, I'm still disappointed in your reckless behavior of running ahead of us." She looked at Tierra. "Now, what do *you* have to say for yourself?"

"Um, that I'm a talented young cat with lots of potential. That I—"

Alada stared at Tierra, unimpressed at her answer.

"That because of how divine I am, I should know better…"

"Well, I hope that you have learned your lesson. I think we should be going now."

Tierra and Birch stood with Alada, though Tierra took point, tail high, eyes scanning the winding path ahead.

A while later, Tierra half-cheered, "This is it!" She stood aside to acknowledge them both. "The end of the not-so-long line! We have officially survived the Lost Labyrinth with only minor personality fragmentation and spiritual confusion!"

They had made it out—but not by luck.

Tierra had stopped joking a few turns back. She'd grown quiet, thoughtful even. Every fork in the path, every echo of the trickster voices, she seemed to feel before it arrived. She didn't guess. She knew.

Now, as they stepped into the pale light of the exit clearing, Alada realized: Tierra had been navigating the whole thing on instinct.

Birch glanced sideways at her. "You didn't even hesitate."

"I listen," Tierra said simply, tapping her head. "To the whispers that want you to fail. And then I walk the opposite way, for one." Regardless of her tactic, she hadn't taken her focus off Birch since she found him.

Hearing this, Birch slowed down and let the two pass him. Something didn't feel right about leaving this place yet. After everything he had endured with the residents of that dreaded place, he felt a connection with them. Gnarla, Moss … trapped within the Labyrinth's many layers of magic. Not everyone in there was out to harm him.

Not everyone is there to help, Birch thought, remembering the flames dancing savagely across Gnarla's branches, their colors like the burning sun setting on the crisp blue waters of the ocean. The demon's malicious grin as she faded into the flames of Gnarla's burning figure…

Get yourself together, Birch. Time to go.

He picked up his pace and caught up to Tierra and Alada (who had completely left the Labyrinth). For them not to notice he had stopped to let them go ahead … didn't feel good. He couldn't release this inner-dread of not being able to help Moss or Gnarla.

A shiver went up his spine as the feeling of being watched

washed over him.

Glancing back one last time, he saw, in the tall grass where he had stood just a few moments ago, a crouched misty version of himself. This ghostly vision looked confused and hopeless, even though the exit was right there. Dumbfounded, Birch stood frozen to the spot; he could only watch the scene play out before him. The ghostly figure sat looking anguished, until a form materialized from the shadows and grabbed its paw.

Moss.

Moss appeared from the mist, silent and steady. He took ghost-Birch's paw without a word, lifted him gently, and together they vanished into the Labyrinth, searching again. Forever lost — but not alone.

Chapter 11
Reality

"Where are we now?" asked Birch, hauling himself over a gargantuan splintered log. "I recall my parents' village being a lot closer."

"The Labyrinth has really screwed up your sense of time. I assure you," Tierra said, turning toward him, "we're almost there. Just beyond this glen."

"Hey, Birch are you alright? I know that labyrinth must have jostled you. Do you need to talk about it at all?" Alada said, stepping closer with genuine concern.

"Who was Gnarla?" asked Tierra. She approached with her shoulders squared, her face serious.

"No one," Birch snapped, trying not to stare at how this cat could do all she does and not get tired. No hair out of line. No sore muscles. No sweat.

"Whoever Gnarla was, I did not hurt her. You have my word." She didn't budge, yet she continued to stare into his eyes. "There are many imitators within that labyrinth. It's dangerous. I get so tired of Meus thinking it a noble quest to send their best warriors into the Labyrinth, as if it's some marker of strength and ability. It's madness. That's all it is. Insanity. No one is capable without proper awareness of what malicious power truly lies within it. I only offered it as an option for us because I would be guiding." Her eyes flashed. Her paws were fists at her side. She turned to Alada. "I'll scout ahead to ensure my direction is clear. Stay and keep watch over Birch. We need to keep a close eye on him until the magic of the Labyrinth wears off."

"When will that be?" Alada asked.

Birch wasn't really listening. He was yet again lost in thought about Gnarla, Moss, and now, his own ghostly figure.

"Probably a few days, honestly. Reality itself will be his cure."

Tierra ran off, leaving Alada standing with Birch. Alada found a flat-ish boulder to sit on nearby as Birch continued to stand until he realized there was no point in standing. He sat straight in the dirt. The birds chirped loudly in the trees and the breeze blew refreshingly cool air.

"What happened to you…" Alada began, "in the Labyrinth? I want to know if you're willing to share. Holly doesn't say much about it." Birch didn't answer. "This was my first time in there, too. I've certainly heard about it.

"You were so against the Labyrinth that it took us a few minutes to realize you may have run right into it. We couldn't believe it at first and trekked a little farther ahead on the path that skirts the Labyrinth before concluding you had, in fact, gone in. That was the only place you could be. Holly said a lot of Meus accidentally get roped into the Labyrinth because they don't know the magical boundaries it has. They think they're outside it when they're not."

No comment. He sighed and, in doing so, remembered Gnarla's drawn-out, exasperated sighs. A grin crossed his face, remembering her, and then it faded instantly. "What do you do when you can't save someone?" he asked woefully. He kicked some pebbles in the dirt. "What do you do when you can't save those that have helped you, but who now need your help?"

Alada was watching a bee collecting pollen from a flower. "That's a thoughtful question," she said. "Let me ponder an equally thoughtful response."

Neither spoke. After a while of kicking pebbles (which honestly kicked up more dust than pebbles), and admiring flowers amidst the obliviously happy chirping of nearby song birds, the sound of someone approaching on foot came to their ears.

Tierra approached quickly, panting only slightly. "Okay, it's somewhat close. We can follow this trail and it will lead us to the east entrance of the village."

Alada rose and stretched, but Birch kept replaying scenes from the Labyrinth in his mind.

"Ouch!" Birch screeched, holding the back of his head. Tierra had rapped him on the head with her water canteen.

"Get out of your head," she commanded.

Why is she so serious suddenly? This Holly seems just as sinister as the version of her I saw hurting Gnarla…

"You must get out of your head. Saying it doesn't seem to be enough. I've said it several times and I don't think you've fully gotten the message. If I see that look again, I will snap you out of it myself. The Labyrinth leaves marks, Birch — and I won't lose another to it." She turned on her heel and led the way down the pebbled path.

Alada made eye contact with Birch as he stood, rubbing his head. "I don't always agree with her, but I do trust she knows the danger signs of those affected by the Labyrinth's spells. She would know them better than anyone. If you're going to trust anyone, trust her right now." She, too, turned on her heel and trailed behind Tierra at a leisurely pace.

A knot formed in Birch's stomach. He did trust Holly … at least he thought he did. But the being in the Labyrinth looked just like her. He trudged along, trying to keep up as his feet felt like lead. *She has done nothing to break my trust.*

He trotted a little faster, trying to catch up to Alada, who had stopped briefly to observe a rare, horned butterfly with its predatorial gold and ruby red wings. *The Labyrinth just lies…*

Alada didn't speak as he approached. "To answer your question, all beings can make mistakes. Sometimes, we can't or weren't meant to save someone," she said solemnly.

"I think accidents or tragedies could be avoided," he said.

"No," she answered, slowly. "That's a control-based per-spective, not a trusting one. Do what you can and accept what you cannot change. No one was meant to have that level of responsibility."

Birch meandered alongside her, thinking. "You ever fail anyone, Jasmine?"

Pause.

"Oh yes."

Pause.

"Me too," he said.

Together, they walked silently as Tierra led the rest of the way.

The small village appeared amidst ancient bioluminescent trees that dwarfed the sleeping village beneath them. A warm, comforting feeling bubbled up and spread through Birch's chest, limbs, and legs. Tierra stood at the village entrance, waiting. When he and Alada arrived, the place appeared to be deserted.

"Where is everyone?" Tierra asked, peeking into a derelict hut nearby. "This place looks like no one has lived here for quite some time."

"No, they're all there," Birch said flatly.

Chapter 12

Stone Creek

Birch walked into the dilapidated hut and opened the moldy curtains, unleashing a considerable cloud of dust and moths. He then walked over to a sagging rust-covered bed and pulled down the sheets, revealing a very old, sleeping Meu, who was the same color as eroded sun-bleached granite.

"Right where I left him," he said, pulling the covers back over the elderly Meu's head.

Next, he padded over to a rickety rocking chair facing the wall where he gently turned it around to face the others. Another elderly Meu, with patchy gray fur, was sitting there, knitting slowly as if she had not yet noticed their presence … or the fact that she had been moved.

Birch tapped her on the paw and spoke in a loud, artic-ulated tone to get her attention. "He-llo, Wood-i-lin. It is very nice to see you again!"

"Woodilin? I have not heard that name in years!" Tierra exclaimed, pleased that the outdated two-hundred-year-old name was still around.

Woodilin looked up from her knitting, showing two very blue and very blind eyes. But she could still knit fairly well. Muscle memory, perhaps?

"Oh, greetings, darling … uh … which one of the Tree family are you again, deary?" she said in a shaky but pleased voice.

Patiently, he knelt down in front of her. "It's me, Birch," he said.

A wide, toothless grin crossed her face. "Birchy, it is so kind of you to visit me and Granite." She reached her paw up and patted him on the head. "My, have you grown since the last time I saw you? You seem so much like your uncle Pine now, so tall."

Birch looked back at Tierra and Alada, and motioned with his head for them to come over. "Woodilin, it is a pleasure to see you again, but there is something important we need to tell you."

"We? Oh, you brought friends! How very delightful of you! May I shake their paw?"

"Of course," Birch said. "Feeling your fur helps her get to know you," he said quietly to Tierra and Alada.

"Okay," Alada said. She reached her paw out and gently shook Woodilin's out-stretched paw, which felt like nothing at all.

Woodilin's expression changed, and though Alada removed her paw, Woodilin kept hers outstretched. It was Tierra's turn to place her paw in the elderly Meu's.

"My, you have some very important cats with you today." She released Tierra's paw in awe.

Birch nodded. "We're on an important mission, that's for sure."

"For what?" she said, straightening up in her weathered rocking chair, which protested with a loud creak.

"To warn everyone of a group that has raided the Central Village."

"Who would want to raid here?" Tierra asked, looking at the dilapidated village surroundings. "This village doesn't need a warning. No one would attack here. They'd arrive and instantly think it was already attacked … ten years ago."

"It was fifteen," Birch corrected her.

"Time flies, doesn't it?" Tierra asked.

"The point is, it's better to know what's coming than not knowing at all," Alada chimed in. "Still could cause a problem for these folks. They don't seem to have much means to defend themselves."

Woodilin stared in her direction once more before turning her attention to Birch for the last time. "Well, thank you, dearie, for the visit. I'll try to wake Granite up soon and tell him the news, and together we can warn the neighbors," she purred in a soft voice.

Birch leaned in and gave the elderly Meu a gentle hug.

"Goodbye, Birch. Say hello to Holly and Cedar for me. Oh, I forgot. Pine and Maple Bark stopped by yesterday and told me they baked cookies. You can have one if you like."

"No, thank you. I wanna get to my parents' house before it gets too late." Birch turned around toward the open door. "Good day, Woodilin. Stay safe."

Tierra and Alada waved and left the broken hut with Birch close behind.

They walked past a few seemingly empty houses before he spoke up. "Sorry that took so long. She loves company, especially since Granite sleeps so much."

Holly's eyes widened with concern. "Why does he sleep so much? Is he sick?"

"Old age, I guess," he said without making eye contact, not looking convinced himself.

They continued walking in silence down the overgrown road, with Birch now leading the way.

Tierra tried to break the silence. "How many Meus live here, exactly?" Although she very well knew how many Meus there were.

Birch paused for a moment and thought on the question, then replied, "I don't quite know. The residents of the area rarely come out for years at a time … or never at all."

Alada, now keen for information about the desolate village of elderly Meus, chimed in next. "How long have your parents lived here?"

"For my whole life. So, for over twenty-five years at least," Birch said, now counting the amorphous huts. "I grew up here. It was my home before I started battle-defense training in the Central Village." He was walking towards a large hut which showcased a little tree-shaped rosewood figure outside the front door.

Alada's face screwed up. "Battle-defense training? The Pyrite Peaks are known for providing the strongest battle-defense training in all of Felina. You know—"

Tierra shot her a look.

"Pyrite Peaks? Do you have a friend there?" Birch asked.

"Of course, I know every — ah … almost everyone well."

Tierra silently slapped her own face. Alada uneasily continued to fix her mistake. It was slightly unusual for a cat to have a friend from another territory, let alone knowing the entire population by name. "And by almost everyone, I actually mean just one Nya named—Snow…shn yar boot … ss. Snowshnyar Boots," Alada finished awkwardly.

Tierra sighed. Out of all the Nyas that she had ever known, Snowshnyar Boots had never even been on the top thousand Nya names ever considered. *Alada's worse than me in making up names on the spot,* Tierra thought, a grin tugging at the corner of her mouth.

To her surprise, Birch actually smiled a bit. "Show shin your boots?" Birch repeated, amused. "I wouldn't want a name like that. Sounds like a tongue twister." He stumbled a bit. "I've never met the Nyas, but if they have names like that, I don't know how well I could keep track of them all."

Looking relieved, Alada looked at Tierra and said, "Well, it's not as unique as FurAhLees, Curry Bees, Hurry Knees, Burry Your Keys, etcetera, etcetera."

"I'd rather have a basic name like Rock or Mud," Birch teased.

They all laughed.

While combing his paw through his messy hair, attempting to straighten it, he said, "Now, enough chat. It is time we say hi."

Chapter 13

Birch's Secret

Are you *sure* this is the right place? Looks like it was already raided ten years ago," a beast snarled.

Another beast shrugged. "If what arrogant black cat said is true, this is the place."

"What now, then?"

The larger beast grunted. "Formation."

"Hellooo…" Birch called as he entered the roomy hut, grinning widely. Inside were two medium beds with home-made blue patchwork quilts in the corner, a small kitchen, and a large cast-iron pot hanging cool over an ash-filled fireplace. Nearer the door stood a rickety, halloh-wood dining table and on it a half-finished puzzle.

Birch's mother and father sat at the table as if they were working on the puzzle together, but the pieces themselves had a layer of dust clearly untouched for many years.

"Hi, mom. Hi, dad," Birch said, still standing in the doorway.

"Birch!" his mom said. "My dear, it's so nice to see you. Come in, come in, come in!" The older she-cat stood, pretending to dust off a chair for him to sit on. "And who are your little friends, Birch?" She eyed Tierra and Alada up and down as if to see if they were worthy of her son's attention.

"This is Holly, and this is Jasmine," Birch said to his parents.

Birch's father hadn't really moved nor noticed the company.

"Cedar," said his mother, "we have company," she said more loudly.

Upon hearing the loud announcement, Cedar slowly turned and looked up to see Tierra and Alada, as Birch stood behind him.

"How did they find us?" Cedar asked, squinting his eyes through cracked spectacles.

"Birch is here, dear," his mother half-shouted. "Birch is here, behind you," she said, touching her husband's left shoulder.

Cedar even more slowly turned to see Birch standing directly behind him. His eyes welled with tears and his chin quivered slightly. Choked up, he said nothing.

"Poor dear hasn't ever gotten over…" his mother began, but quickly fell silent. She turned her attention directly to Tierra and Alada. "My husband suffers from a delusion. He thinks … well, it's not really important right now. It's so lovely you're visiting. Please, please. Sit and share what you've all been up to."

Tierra and Alada took seats opposite Cedar and as with his son, he said nothing to either of them.

Is that jealousy in his eyes? Tierra thought. *Longing? Why is he staring so much?*

Cedar didn't seem to have an ounce of social etiquette, staring at strangers the way he was. He sat there, unblinking, and each time Tierra or Alada averted their eyes, he merely stared at the other until she got so uncomfortable as to avert her eyes, to which he'd switch back and look at the other.

"We're here on business, Mom," Birch said. "We won't be staying beyond a night."

Birch's mother's eyes filled instantly with tears. "You don't want to stay? But it's been so long since you've been home!"

Birch's discomfort was palpable as he shifted in his chair, which squeaked on the wooden floor.

"I'll make your favorite dinner tonight," she said, folding her hands in her lap. "I would love to get to know each of you," she added, focusing her attention on Tierra and Alada. "It's so nice to see Birch with friends. Now, I don't want to be too forward, but Birch is getting older, and maybe one of you could talk him in to settling down." Her words were more poignant now, and she stared, unblinkingly, at them both. "And have a family."

Tierra and Alada found themselves staring down at their lap.

"We would be glad to share some about ourselves," Tierra soon said. "Thank you for hosting us for tonight. We have an important mission and Birch wanted to be sure we stop by."

"My Birch is so thoughtful," his mother said.

"What is your name?" Alada asked. "You haven't said yet."

His mother blushed a bit. "Holly." She made eye contact with Tierra, who knew very well that she was name comparing with her. "Maybe not so much a coincidence for my dear son. We always had a close relationship. Very respectful young Meu." She pinched his cheek, which he tried to dodge.

"Mom, there was an attack on the Central Village. We are visiting from village to village to warn you all," Birch said, deliberately driving the conversation away from the cheek-pinching, please-marry-my-son topics.

His mother stared. "Attacks on the other villages?"

"Yes, Mom. We needed to stop here on the way to the larger village several miles from here. This was a great opportunity to see you and rest up before heading out. This is the safest place I could think of visiting that no one would look for us."

His mother nodded. "This is a safe place. We rarely get visitors anymore. We just stick to ourselves." She looked at Cedar, who still continued to stare uncomfortably at Tierra and Alada. "It does get a little lonely. So, it's lovely to have you here for even a short while." She got up and pretended to open the door to let in fresh air. The windows were already open, with no shutters, and thick cobwebs adorned every crevice and corner.

"Such an important mission, isn't it, Cedar?" she announced. Cedar didn't move a muscle.

Birch made to speak again, but a loud, familiar roar echoed throughout the village. Looking out the window, he saw a half-dozen beasts standing together in the center of the dilapidated town.

"Guests?" asked his mother. "We'd love guests! Oh, how wonderful!" His mother stood and made way to welcome the newcomers.

"We need to hide," Birch said, motioning to Tierra and Alada toward the back wall. "Be quiet." He opened a small closet and shoved them inside while squeezing himself in amidst their breathless, I-can't-breathe protests.

"Are you sure this place hasn't been torched already?" asked a beast from beside his quiet leader. He scanned the small town. "Looks deserted."

The leader remained silent, observing.

"Maybe the other platoon scorched it and killed 'em all," growled another. "A waste of time!"

"Round them up," growled the leader. "Find them all. Search every home."

The beasts half-strode, half-trotted away, yelling loudly as if to intimidate and scare any inhabitants into submission.

The leader strode to the farthest hut to which he thought he saw a face peeking out moments before. He wasted no time and began busting down the door, which in the door's dilapidated state had easily given way and merely stuck around his extended foot. The leader breathed in deeply, with the intent to let out a ferocious roar, only to cough uncontrollably from the dust and mold he had sent into the air upon his entrance.

"Welcome!" his mother, Holly, had said. "Cedar! Look! Company!"

Cedar simply turned to stare at the enormous beast who had broken down his door. "Uh huh," he moaned, unimpressed.

"GET OUT!" the leader roared, half-wheezing.

"But I just made cakes," said Birch's mother. "Would you like some? Oh! Here," she added, "I have some tea on the kettle. Perhaps some tea would help with your cough. I can't imagine why you would be out when you have a cough. In my day," she said, bustling about to clear a seat strong enough for this beast. "In my day, we didn't go out if we had a cough, so we wouldn't spread it to others. I call it common decency, but you know," she went about looking for a non-cob-webbed teacup, "I guess these newer generations merely want to be out and busy no matter how they feel."

The leader merely stared at these Meus, who didn't seem to care at all about his threats or menacing presence.

"I SAID GET OUT!" he yelled again, but Birch's mother paid no mind really, nor did Cedar even so much as flinch.

"We're always getting out with the fresh air," Birch's mother replied. "Perhaps that would do your cough some good. In fact, I heard that air filled with mold can cause long-term lung issues. Do you live in a moldy place?" she asked, sitting back in her own chair. "You look like a strapping young man. Perhaps you could stay and help Cedar repair the roof?"

"STOP TALKING!" the leader demanded. "We're rounding you all up and are gonna burn your town to the ground unless you all decide to be under the control of our leader!"

"So, you're not a leader?" asked Cedar.

"I am the leader of this platoon," growled the beast.

"But you're not an *actual* leader," said Cedar. "You're not THE leader. You're just A leader. Big difference." He looked the leader up and down. "I'm not impressed. Do you need a tissue?"

The leader felt his face flush with fury and as he stood over Cedar, he heard the other beasts yell in the distance. Quickly exiting the house, he saw the gracious villagers had inundated his platoon — eager for them to share a meal or have a chat. The villagers feared nothing.

"What is this craziness?" roared the leader, looking around as nothing in the village had burned. "Why aren't you rounding them up?" he screeched.

"We can't!" howled a beast who ran up quickly. "This village … this village!" he said, stuttering all the way. "We have to leave! Never come back!"

Tierra and Alada thought perhaps it was the sticky sweetness of the villagers that may have repulsed the beasts into retreat. Emerging from a secret nook behind the beds, it was clear something else had also frightened the beasts into leaving.

The fading yells that now echoed were that of the beasts as they tried to gather themselves up and get enough distance from the villagers to glitch away. With great effort, the beasts glitched away as they ran, almost scattering to the outskirts of town.

Tierra and Alada didn't know what to say as they stood in the hut. They never thought that sugary sweetness would fend off these horrible creatures. Confused and at a loss for words, they observed Birch's mother and Cedar, who were acting as though nothing out of the ordinary had happened at all.

"I can't believe how fearless you all are," Alada said, sitting down opposite Cedar, now looking at him in the eyes.

"It's easy," said Cedar, disgruntled.

Birch abruptly coughed in a not-actually-coughing-but-need-your-attention sort of way. "Can I speak with you both outside?" Alada and Tierra followed Birch outside and into the woods a short distance from the hut.

"That was incredible," said Tierra. "I really don't know what to say. Maybe these beasts can scare off more easily than we thought?"

Birch's emotionless face now looked pained. "It's not the sweetness…"

"What do you mean?" asked Alada. "The beasts were clearly uncomfortable with the attention and kindness they were getting."

Birch shifted uncomfortably, almost as if wanting out of his own skin.

"Seriously, if we pass along the information that they are beaten with generosity and kindness, which is a little cliché–" said Tierra.

"Really?" asked Birch, flatly.

"What?"

"They're dead, Holly."

Alada stood closer to Tierra. "What do you mean?" asked Alada. "What do you mean they're 'dead'? They look just like us."

Birch merely stood, staring. "They're all dead."

Silence prevailed.

"They just either don't know it or haven't accepted it. The only one who has done either … is my dad. The rest are in denial."

Birds chirped, frogs croaked, and insects made noises filling the silence.

"You're going to explain, right?" Tierra asked. "It seems obvious a story of explanation needs to be inserted here because we have nothing to say."

Birch gave Tierra a look that was neither funny nor amused.

"When I was an older child, our village was attacked and burned. All but five Meus survived, including myself; the other survivors were also young. I survived by hiding in the very closet we were just in to protect ourselves from these beasts. After the attack, it was clear how many had fallen, and we wanted to bury the dead, but there were too many bodies, and the ghosts of those who had fallen began appearing in droves. Unnerved by the presence of the dead villagers, three of the five of us survivors fled. They were neighbor kittens I used to play with. I've never seen them again. Myself and one other Meu tried to live here as long as we could. Her name was Willow, and she was supposed to be my betrothed." Birch clearly lost himself in remembrance.

"Aaannnd…?" prompted Tierra.

"And we soon discovered that we couldn't live in an undead town of ghosts. She left first, heading for the small village of Enoki Hallow, where she had aunts and uncles." He dabbed his left eye with his right knuckle as he tried to stifle a shuddered breath. "I didn't want to leave." Birch's eyes welled with tears as he stared, fixedly, at the ground. "I love my parents and my town, but I soon realized I couldn't live that way either. I can't touch my parents for real. They're stuck in a loop. So, I visit once a year as if I moved away as all Meus do — playing along with the vision that they're still alive."

"But what happens when you're older than they are?" Alada asked. "We need to help them."

"Not right now, though, we're on another mission after all," Tierra interjected. "Another time, but I agree the town needs help."

Birch semi-nodded. "I tried for years to help them understand what had happened. Only my father could come to understand the reality, but it took a few years. He still hasn't fully accepted it."

"So now he lives in a village where he knows the truth and no one else does," Alada said. "That's difficult."

Birch nodded his head.

"So, we're going to sleep in a haunted village," Tierra said … flatly.

Birch nodded. "It's not really that bad. It's easy to pretend they're all alive, they fooled you two after all."

"It still doesn't change the fact that we now *know* we're sleeping in a haunted village," said Tierra.

Alada interjected, as Tierra was clearly unsettled.

"Look, Birch. It's not that we don't like your parents. They seem like lovely Meus. I think Holly is just … a little … taken by the surprise," Alada said, slowly and carefully.

"When were you going to tell us?" Tierra spat.

Birch frowned. "They aren't dangerous. They just want to be loved and helpful."

"We're not saying anything contrary. They're lovely," Alada added.

"Your dad stares," Tierra said. "But he seems nice," she added. "I like how he tells it like it is. Like how he told that beast that he was unimpressed with him being a leader." Tierra smiled. "That was pretty exceptional."

"It's just one night," Birch said. "My parents stay up all night. They'll just make tea, sit by the fireplace seeing flames though it's unlit and whatnot. They'll be quiet. They're used to me visiting."

Tierra seemed slightly angst at this revelation, though no one knew why, as it seemed not such a big deal … ish.

"Why did we come here to warn them if they're already dead when we've got towns filled with living people to protect?"

Birch's hackles silently stiffened and raised to which Tierra stumbled on what to say next. While she agreed with her own claim, somehow, it felt inappropriate.

Thankfully, Alada piped in before Birch or Tierra spoke again. "We needed to venture this way anyway to reach the other larger villages. We can't see them all and this is a great rest stop. If this place were attacked, ghosts or not, they are unaware they are dead and it may scare them. They still have feelings."

Watching a trail of ants on a small fallen log a short distance from her foot, Tierra nodded with an awkward cough. "Yes, of course. That makes sense."

Satisfied enough, Birch walked back to the village to visit with the others, as everyone, ghosts or not, were always eager for visitors.

Once Birch was out of earshot, Tierra instantly looked up. "Are you telling me you're okay with this? Staying in this undead village?"

"Yes," Alada said, resolution in her voice. "Who else has had the opportunity to spend a couple of days in a pleasantly haunted village?" She pointed to the untouched, natural beauty around them and the pleasant nearby chatter of ghostly neighbors going about their day. "This has so far proven to be, and can continue to be, a really interesting, positive experience," Alada said, giving a genuine smile.

"Since they're nice and kind, I think we're safe to explore. Certainly uncharted territory, eh?" She patted Tierra on the shoulder as she, too, began to saunter back toward the old huts and houses.

Tierra straggled behind, following at a short distance.

"Yes, it is nice to be back," Birch said to his neighbor, an elderly Meu who squinted constantly. "No, no, I haven't married yet."

The little old Meu continued to query Birch's living and life habits while Alada and Tierra stood idly by. As Birch made his farewells to Ms. Squint, he returned to Alada's and Tierra's side, yet said nothing.

Within moments, Alada broke the silence. "They're really lovely Meus. I can see why you didn't want to leave."

Nothing had changed, really. The village mostly looked deserted and ghostly Meus only occasionally walked here and there.

"They were attacked in the night," Birch remarked, observing the vacant village. "That's why so many can still be found in their beds." He shuffled his paws. "Some have never left their beds; others have gotten up to go about their day."

"I still don't understand how they don't know they're dead," Tierra said. "They don't eat or drink or sleep."

"Denial," Birch said flatly. "That's all. Don't complicate it. It's simple."

"Birch!" called his mother. "Time to come in for supper!"

"What do ghosts like to read?" Tierra asked aloud.

"Boooooks."

Birch didn't yell. He spun on his heel — a full one-eighty, in more ways than one. "Don't joke about them." His voice was low, grave, and filled with something ancient.

Tierra had momentarily frozen on the spot.

"Er, Birch?" said Alada, "Holly is uncomfortable. And while I agree she should not make jokes, jokes may be how she copes with disquieting situations." She looked from Tierra to Birch. "I want you two to be clear about why you're behaving the way you are, so you don't become enemies. Respect and understanding from both parties is required if we are to continue on this mission *together*." She stood next to Tierra, putting a paw on her frozen shoulder.

"You had no trouble with the spirits and ghosts of the Lost Labyrinth, I'm sure you can sleep well here knowing we don't have to worry about ghosts with malicious intent."

Tierra shook her head slightly, but still did not speak as Birch continued to stare down at her with a seriousness she had never witnessed before. She had crossed a line. Once he departed to pick some vegetables, they turned toward one another.

"These are *real* ghosts," Tierra whispered.

"Yes … what of it?"

"The Lost Labyrinth is not what it seems."

Alada stood there, waiting. "Annnd? What of that?"

"The Labyrinth is filled with reflections of interactive memories … for one."

Alada shook her head as if trying to make sense of what

she said. "That doesn't make sense. It's known for being filled with ghosts."

Tierra bobbed her head. "Yes, and no. None of us, none of the Guardians, know all there is to know about that place. That's why I learned to get in and get out quickly. I'm not joking when I say getting lost is serious business."

"But joking about these *real* deceased loved ones is acceptable?" Alada's frow furrowed.

Tierra glowered toward the nearest tree.

"Not everything is fun and games, Tierra," Alada said. "Parties and games are fun because they're not constantly occurring. They're once in a while. This is not the time for either."

Tierra merely cast her eyes down to the ground, once again saying nothing. They turned back toward the village, and at the request of Birch's mother, they all entered the family hut.

"Birch, dear," said his mother. "I would love your help preparing dinner," she said as she busied herself with the movements of washing dishes and wiping down the counter. "Would you please gather ingredients for dinner? Only worry about yourselves. I hardly feel hungry anymore. Your father and I barely nibble much these days." She patted her husband on the shoulder. "Still a strapping husband!" she said, smiling at Cedar, who barely lifted one side of this mouth in a type of half-smile acknowledgment.

"And you don't look a day beyond thirty-seven," Cedar replied. "Oh, wait…" he spoke with a slight sarcasm in his tone.

Birch's mother scowled at the compliment.

"The compliment always starts off so lovingly, yet then you bring up your silly theory and turn it into an insult," hissed Birch's mother.

"Just the truth, dear," Cedar said, staring at the table.

"Would you like to go for a walk, Mr. uh…. Birch's dad?" Alada asked, standing near the door. "It's lovely this time of evening. We can get some fresh air while Birch makes dinner."

For once, Cedar turned his head and stared, unblinking, as uncomfortably as always, toward Alada, who slowly began to regret the offer.

"They don't really do many different activities," Birch remarked, softly. "Dad hasn't left that chair for many years…"

Cedar got up and walked out the door without so much as a word. Birch stared wide-eyed after his father. Alada, clearly uncomfortable, walked after Cedar anyway. As if in a trance himself, Birch followed, leaving Tierra "Holly" to stand alone with his mother, Holly.

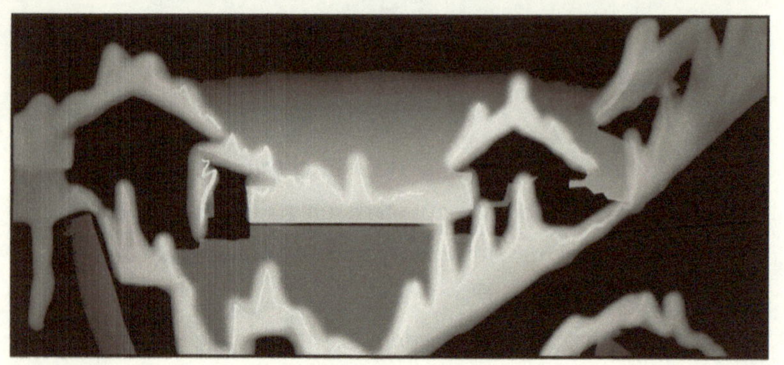

Chapter 14
That Night

Cedar was outside, something Birch hadn't seen in fifteen years.

"Let's go along this wooded path," Alada remarked. "We can go to the meadow where I saw the sunlight coming through the branches earlier. It was stunning."

Cedar followed silently. Alada periodically felt a shiver up her spine each time she noticed how she only heard the crunching leaves under her own paws and that of Birch from the far back. Yet, there were three of them. He walked toward the edge of the trees, steps silent on the grass, as if the earth made no sound for the dead.

The meadow, indeed, had a welcoming warmth and calm serenity about it. Birds quietly chirped from the trees. The sun shone through the branches, casting almost rainbow-like hues across the tall grasses. Alada found a flat boulder to sit upon. Birch continued to stand near his father, though not too close. Minutes passed. An hour passed as they watched the light show of the meadow's waving grasses.

"I'm going to gather some food for dinner," Birch said softly. "I'll check back soon."

Alada turned her head and smiled with a brief nod. Soon after Birch's pawsteps faded away, the silence once again reigned. She closed her eyes, taking in the sounds that echoed in her perfect ears.

"It was a terrible night," Cedar croaked.

Alada opened her eyes but did not speak. Cedar had not moved or budged or even turned his head to look at her when he spoke. He solely looked in one direction: forward.

"It had been a peaceful evening. We just had a community dinner. Birch was difficult to get to sleep that night because he had been running around with his friends right before bedtime. He wanted to go fishing with me that night. He tried to convince me to grab our poles and sneak out when Mom fell asleep…" He sighed heavily. "But I said no. Not tonight." Cedar's voice trailed off and on as if reliving an experience more than retelling it. "If we left, I would have lived. My presence made no difference. Everyone died anyway." He stood silently for a moment and went on. "I went to bed and immediately woke up to screams that seemed as if they would never end." His voice began to crack and strain. "I shoved Birch into the hidden closet half-asleep. I grabbed my staff and a sword my father had given to me, and ran outside. The village was ablaze, so we all could see every detail of our own destruction with the utmost clarity. I tried to fight, but I couldn't take them all on. Soon, with each passing moment, the sounds of screams faded … and faded … and faded … to silence." His eyes were large, un-blinking. Even from her seat, Alada could see tears welled in his eyes. "The silence … the silence … there was nothing like… that silence."

Alada found that she, herself, was not blinking. By the time she realized her mouth had drooped open, she blinked hard as her eyes were quite dry.

"If you had lived, would you have forgiven yourself for not being there to fight?" Alada asked. "You wouldn't have known you would have all died. Would you have thought you could have made a difference?"

Cedar abruptly turned his head toward her, which startled her so greatly she jumped a little.

"No one has ever asked me that," he said. "I've never thought of that. I've only known what happened. Like a loop…"

"You are clearly a loving father and husband," she said slowly. "Would you have blamed yourself all these years had you gone fishing?" she whispered.

Cedar heaved with each breath. "A fate worse than death … yes."

Thankfully, he stopped staring so intensely into her eyes and turned back to observe the meadow once again.

"Would you have even been able to leave your wife if you had lived?"

She could see his eyes widen, and a few minutes passed in the usual silence.

"No … I never would have been able to leave … alive."

Silence once again prevailed and was left undisturbed until the padding paws of Birch's reemergence rang in their ears.

"Dinner is ready," Birch said to Alada. "Dad, are you ready to come home for dinner?"

As per character, Cedar silently pulled his attention away from the meadow, almost reluctantly, to quietly follow his son back to the hut. Alada padded along behind.

Back at home, Birch's mother apparently had been chatting nonstop to Tierra about gardening. Tierra's eyes looked slightly glossed over as they all entered and sat around the now cleared and dusted dining table and chairs.

"Did you have an enjoyable walk?" asked Tierra, slightly interrupting Birch's mother's description of a simple watering system utilizing seven buckets, hollow branches, and a knife. Cedar had sat himself back in his chair, and once again fixed his gaze on the tabletop.

"Yes," Alada noted. "We spent a while watching the meadow during the sunset. It was lovely out this evening."

Birch brought over the food he had collected on one large, clean platter. "It's beets, wild ginger, wild onion, wild carrots, wild mushrooms, apples, berries, and lettuce."

"What makes only the ginger, onion, carrots, and mushrooms wild and not the other foods?" asked Tierra. "Do they like to go on dangerous adventures? Yell and scream into the night and dance around fires?"

Birch's mother laughed. "Oh, Holly, dear, such a sense of humor. A fine quality in a young Meu," she said sweetly, while looking directly into Birch's eyes.

Alada noticed the hint and smirked into her cup of water.

Birch blushed, flashing a glance at Tierra before looking down at the platter of food in the center of the table. "This isn't centered," he said, edging the platter a nudge to the right. "There. Now, uh, Dad, how did you like the meadow?"

Since he never answered anyway, Birch's mother began in again about how, on warm evenings like this one, she liked to go and weed the garden.

"I had forgotten about it," Cedar said.

Everyone turned to face him. And patiently waited.

No one knew what to say. What do you say to a ghost who's remembering … memories?

"I saw a time where I taught Birch to fly his first kite," Cedar said. "I saw the boulder on the forest edge where Holly and I got married under the sacred oak."

Birch's mother's mouth had drooped open.

Several minutes passed where Cedar remained silent.

"So, um, what do you and Cedar like to do in your spare time?" Tierra asked.

Birch's mother wasted no time diving into her knitting habits and showing the sample she was clearly, and had been clearly, working on for the past twenty years.

"Fishing," Cedar said.

Birch's mouth dropped open. "Mine too."

Cedar peered over at Birch.

"We could go in the morning before you leave," Cedar said.

Birch stumbled about for words. "I would like that."

After a skip of a beat, Birch's mother chimed in happily. "Well, if you two are going fishing in the early, we best eat up and get you three off to bed." She turned to Tierra and Alada. "I hope you two don't mind sharing the larger of the two beds. I'll fluff the pillows and blankets before you get into it."

"It's okay, Mom, I'll do it. You should rest," said Birch. He jogged a few paces and grabbed the quilts off the two beds before carefully and slowly walking them out to the front yard so as not to fling dust around. Once outside, he put one quilt down on a small splintered fence and began flinging the other one around in the air, trying to get as much dust off as possible.

"I'll help!" called Alada, darting outside to grab the other end. "Here, can we beat it against a tree?"

Tierra watched from within as Birch's mother merely smiled at her some more. "So, dear, how old are you?" she said, sitting down in a rocking chair by the fireless fireplace.

"Oh, uh…" Honestly, she had forgotten. "Oh, how old is Birch?" Tierra felt her palms beginning to sweat. *When will they be done beating the quilts?* She glanced toward the front door.

"Gosh, I suppose around twenty-six?" his mother replied, working on her knitting once again. "Time feels different these days. Sometimes, it's difficult to keep track!"

"Oh, well," Tierra said, coughing to stall for time, "Twenty-five. No, twenty-four. I like that number."

Birch's mother smiled a toothy grin in Tierra's direction.

"How nice that you like the number of your age. I hope you can like all the ages you become. Time is so fast and youth so fleeting." She had paused for only a hair's breath. "Do you know if you and Birch have much in common? He likes so many things. I'm sure you must have *something* in common."

"Uh, well." The awkward moment made every second feel like a year by comparison. "We both care about the villages and want to help others. We only just met, a day ago — yesterday. No, two days ago? So, we haven't had a chance to see what else we have in common."

"Here we go," Birch announced upon his re-entry. "I'll do the pillows next."

"No! Let me help. I love helping. It's the best in the world," Tierra spoke with incredible speed, to which she grabbed all the pillows her arms could hold and left the room as fast as her legs could go.

Birch followed, carrying a pillow she had dropped.

"We're hitting them here, right?" Tierra asked, trying to balance pillows on the makeshift garden fence.

"We can beat them on the smooth bark tree over here," said Alada, eyeing Tierra's scattered energy and wide eyes.

"Mom talking to you about me, huh?" came Birch's amused voice. "Sorry. I've never brought anyone here before, so she must think this means something."

Tierra felt her face relax. "That makes a lot of sense." She grabbed a pillow and walked over to beat it on the smooth bark.

"I hope you both can find it more amusing than annoying," he continued, taking the freshly dusted pillows and handing them the dusty ones.

"Yeah," said Tierra. "Come to think of it, I have been feeling that it's rather amusing. Annoying never came to mind at all." She sneaked a peek at Birch as she handed him a dusted pillow. He handed her a dusty one with a smile. His kind eyes were somehow gleaming in the newfound moonlight.

"Your mother's adoration is quite endearing," Alada remarked, hitting a pillow particularly hard on the bark, accidentally tearing a small hole, sending bits of feathers into the air. "Oops! I'm so sorry!"

"No worries," he said, taking the torn pillow. "This one has been falling apart for years."

"I notice how she doesn't interrogate *you*," Tierra stated, looking at Alada.

"I'm too old," Alada said, laughing. Being the eldest of the Guardians, she had seen a few dozen … centuries. Only Tierra would get the inside joke.

"You're not too old," Birch said, bringing out his masculine chivalry. He knew why his mother was giving personalized attention to Tierra, and it wasn't about age. "You don't look a day over…" Alada shot him an amused and somewhat theatrically offended glance at this momentary pause. "Seventeen," he said awkwardly, as he caught her eye.

Alada merely smiled. "I believe your mother has a particular interest in someone who shares her name. What do you think, *Holly?*" She fancied a teasing glance to Tierra, who couldn't help but snicker as she beat out a cloud of dust from a pillow.

Birch remained silent, pretending to organize the … single pillow in his arm. Should he hold it horizontally? No, vertical? Maybe spin it a few times … find the right balance.

"Well," Tierra announced, holding the last now dusted pillow, "at least we won't breathe dust in every time we roll over. I'm sure the mattresses are just as dusty, but the clean pillows and quilts will do."

"I agree," said Alada, holding hers to her chest.

"I never had a problem. I always found this sufficient." Birch walked away back toward the house and walked in without waiting for them.

With a sly glance at one another, they both reentered the home and tucked into the same bed, with the kind "good nights" of his mother calling out to them.

When Alada looked over to wish Tierra a goodnight, she found her already asleep. "I knew you would sleep anywhere," she said. "Sleep well."

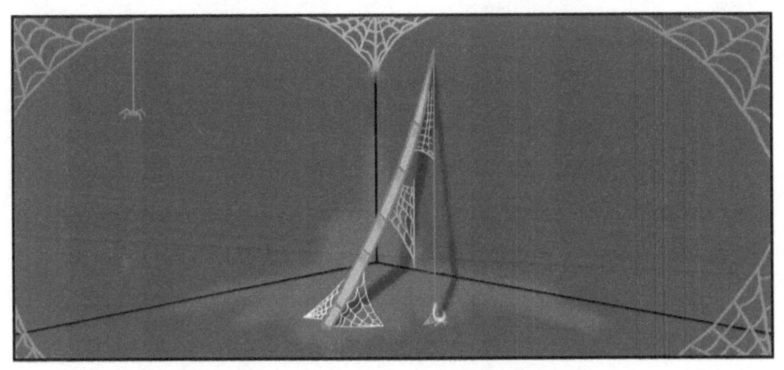

Chapter 15
Fishing

When Birch awoke in the early, early morning, he found his father sitting at the table and his mother knitting by the nonexistent fire, as usual.

The bed creaked under his weight as he shifted out, now groggily approaching his father. The windows had been left open. He hugged himself a bit to warm up. *Would Dad remember saying he wanted to go fishing?*

"Yes, we can go," Cedar said quietly. "Your mother won't notice if we're gone for a few hours." Birch's mother hadn't acknowledged him and in fact, hadn't noticed any movement within the hut. Cedar continued, "Grab the pole. You can also grab some leftovers from last night's dinner as bait."

As Birch fetched the dust and cobweb-covered fishing pole, a memory sparked from the last time he had touched it. It was he who had put the pole there fifteen years ago after a successful fishing trip with his dad. His heart swelled with joy at the memory. He could have fished with him every day and been happy.

They walked outside together and silently padded over to the almost-dried pond. The water had receded from the dock quite a way, but Cedar sat on its edge like he used to.

Birch sat beside him, baited the pole and cast off into a lone puddle some feet away. His insides crunched around as it reminded him of how he tried to live among his parents for a few years … but couldn't. It was never the same — like living in a painful memory of what once was.

"I'm sorry, Birch," Cedar said after a half hour.

Birch recast, trying to reach a farther puddle. "For what?"

"For … dying. For not going fishing with you. For not being the dad I should have been. For knowing had I lived, I still would have died feeling like I failed your mom."

Birch recast to fill space while his thoughts raced, and his heart skipped several beats.

Cedar sat there, his whiskers twitching periodically as he continued his soliloquy. "For being stuck here. For being stuck wandering this world beyond your lifespan …"

Birch recast yet again trying to aim for the patch of pond beyond the thread-length of the pole. He let silence sit before saying, "When I die, will I be a ghost?"

For once, Cedar looked at him. "No." There was no question or concern in his voice.

"Then why are you all ghosts?" asked Birch, feeling anger tighten in his throat. "Will I just die and move on, and we're still stuck apart because I'm not a ghost and you still are? Are we always going to just be slightly out of touch forever?" He could hear the volume of his voice raising as his chest tightened.

Cedar breathed in deeply and sighed.

"Why do you even breathe if you're dead?" asked Birch, as he put down his pole. "Why do you choose to remain a ghost if you know the truth? Why can't you just move on?"

"I will not always be a ghost. And you will never be one. How this comes to be, I do not know, but I have a strong sense …" he looked over his shoulder, speaking slowly, "that your friends will be the ones to help us figure that out. And," Cedar said, taking another deep breath, "you are always breathing. You exhale from your physical body and inhale into your spiritual body. It's that simple. Don't complicate it."

At that, Birch's ears twitched, and something in him eased. For once, his father was actually talking in a familiar way. For once, since his death, he could hear the father he once knew. Though they sat mostly in silence, the speckled conversation throughout their fishing time was easy and light, and he felt a rekindling spark of connection he thought had been lost. After a while, with no catches of the day, they quietly walked back to the hut. Birch noticed himself stepping with a strange lightness in his paws.

Tierra and Alada were both outside the hut alongside Birch's mother when they approached. Both looked semi-rested, but Tierra looked outright eager to get going as she kept stepping closer toward the woods.

"Now, dear, you should visit more often, dear," Birch's mother said, pinching Birch on the cheek. "And hopefully, next time, you'll come with someone *special*," she said again, smiling at Tierra and Alada. "You have lovely company."

"Thanks, Mom. We appreciate staying the night to rest up," Birch said quickly. "We'll be in touch. I always visit."

"Yes, but please consider settling down soon," his mother went on.

"Thanks, Dad, for fishing with me," Birch said, facing his father, who stood by the empty vegetable patch. Cedar nodded a little and then nodded toward Tierra and Alada.

"It was lovely to meet you two lovely Meus," Birch's mother said, waving gently at Tierra and Alada. "Such pretty Meus, too. Son, be sure to protect them and take care of them during your adventure. Birch was always the strongest leader of all his friends," she said, patting his arm. He barely dodged another cheek-pinch.

"Mom, thank you, but we need to go. There are a lot of villages to warn."

"Yes, yes. I know. Okay, dear, take care. Blessings on your journey!" She waved cheerfully as they set out.

As Birch looked back, he met his father's gaze and, with another nod from him, turned and headed in the only direction life has: forward.

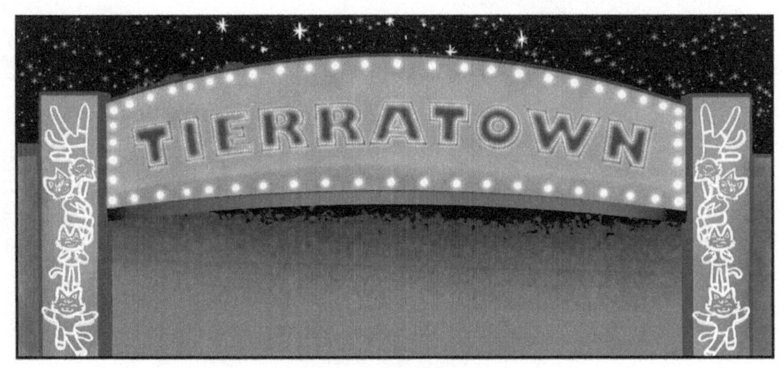

Chapter 16

Tierra Town!

What's the next town we're going to?" Birch asked from the back of the pack.

"Map says Tierra Town," Alada said, eyeing Tierra. "Your family's town isn't even on the map anymore, Birch." She stopped and stared at him. "What if we put it back on the map? They could finally have visitors … like a living historical site. Or a positive ghost visitation experience. I'm sure it could be worked in a compassionate way."

"No," Birch answered. "No way. They're not attractions on display."

"They're lonely," Alada said. "Lonely ghosts."

Birch walked around her, ignoring her statements.

"Tierra Town," Tierra said to Birch, brightly, "is a great place. You're going to love it. It's definitely on my list of the top five best towns." Birch remained silent, but Tierra marched on, talking loudly. "These fern tops are great snacks. It's good to pick them off as we walk for more energy. That way, maybe we'll stop less and make it there before nightfall."

"It's a two-day walk, Holly," Alada pointed out on the map.

Tierra brushed off the fact with a wave of her paw. "We could get there by nightfall if we don't stop, so let's keep going. We can do it! Just keep eating these fern heads."

"Holly!" Alada said, raising her voice. "We are not arriving by nightfall by ingesting fern heads!"

Tierra sighed in a dramatically loud fashion. "Well, let's see how far we can get anyway, no harm done in that."

"I could probably keep up this time," Birch chimed in. "These ferns are pretty good actually."

"Yeah! And the occasional nut we find," Tierra enthusiastically replied, "will be just the ticket!"

Alada slapped her forehead with her paw.

Strangely enough—and to Alada's dismay—the sounds of the town began echoing through the woods just before nightfall. The ground reverberated beneath their feet, the vibrations rising with every step. The music grew louder and louder, until Alada could almost make out the lyrics. They were still a good distance away, yet the neon lights already flashed across the trees, making the forest feel like it had a heartbeat… a very rhythmic, rock-concert sort of heartbeat—but a heartbeat nonetheless.

"See? We made it! Extra points for those four berries Birch found just beyond the path an hour ago," Tierra said, turning to give him a you-did-it smile. "Wow! I can smell the confetti cannons now," Tierra said with a nostalgic sigh. "Now let's go in and get this party STARTED!"

"Party?" Alada asked.

"Of course, there are always parties in Tierra Town. They give out free custom Tierra-themed party hats for all newcomers! Tierra hospitality is the best you can get in all of Felina! Free drink! Free food! Free Tierra hairstyling!"

"Food?" Birch said, his eyes wide with craving. "Sounds good to me!"

"Tierra hairstyling? There's only one hairstyle here?" Alada asked flatly.

"Yup." Tierra flicked her hair with her paw. "Medium length, wavy at the ends, the color of autumn blush-roses, and blows magically in the wind."

"Yes, but about the food!" Birch could smell the wonderous aroma of something sticky, maybe cinnamon? Maybe toast? Whatever it was, he wanted twelve. Thoughts of all things sweet and sticky dripping over his fingers burst like a fantasy bubble when he noticed Tierra eyeing his and Alada's hair with a calculating gaze.

He noticed that the fur on Tierra's head was suddenly much longer than it had been an hour ago, now falling well below her shoulders. "When did you get such long hair?" he asked, thoroughly confused.

Tierra grinned—a somewhat alarmingly toothy grin.

"Glad you asked! Just fur extensions. I always carry a few with me. Wanted to get festive. Want to try? I've got extras—blue, green, even glitter-tipped!"

Birch stared at her, quietly hoping he would not be expected to get festive too. "I'm getting the sense that you really like Tierra and her town," he said.

"Yup! Now, come on!" she said excitedly. "I want you two to get settled in before the fireworks start."

Birch and Alada looked at each other in bewilderment. "Fireworks?" they said at once. "But, we have to warn –" But all they got for an answer was Tierra roughly grabbing their wrists and dragging them to the gates.

The gates to Tierra Town were quite an uncommon sight. The frame of the gate was tall and thin, with tiny neon Tierras painted around the edges in all kinds of poses. Hanging below the gate was a gigantic sign that read: Tierra Town!

Guarding the entrance were two Meus who looked so much like Holly that Birch did a double-take. One was more graceful and elegant than Tierra herself — like an idealized, feline portrait of her. The other looked like Tierra if she were a strapping young male, broad-shouldered and confident, with flowing hair.

They leaned against the walls on either side of the doors. One seemed half asleep, while the other talked non-stop to the other, seemingly unaware of the fact that he was not listening.

"Hiya! Dierra, Kierra! How's the guarding? Seen any party crashers lately?" Tierra exclaimed as she dragged Alada and Birch forward.

When the one named Dierra heard her, she gasped, immediately ran over, and gave Tierra a big hug, who involuntarily released Alada and Birch.

"Holly, Holly, Holly! Oh my gosh, you're here! The Hip-Hop-Tierra-Pop Dance-off battle is like going to start—like *soooo* soon! Kierra, get over here — it's Holly!" Dierra said, hopping up and down all the while.

Kierra, woken up by Dierra's sudden loudness, drowsily stumbled over to the group.

"Hiya, hiya, everyone. Whatsup? Holl' and all ready to dance? The H.H.T.P Dance-off should happen with you 'round," Kierra said.

Alada was quite confused. "Why with Holly around?"

Dierra scoffed in disbelief. "Every Meu knows that whenever Holly is around, Tierra is close behind!"

Alada glared at Tierra. "Oh right, she sure is."

Turning her attention back to Tierra, she said, "Now, who are they? Not from here, I'd guess."

"Oh yeeeah," Tierra murmured. She was so eager to party she had forgotten to introduce her companions. "This is Jasmine and this is Birch."

Dierra and Kierra's eyes widened with interest. "Is he going to be your partner for the dance-off?" Dierra purred.

"No!" both Tierra and Birch said together. Birch blushed and looked everywhere else. *Is that leaf on the tree crooked?*

Kierra glanced up at the moon to check the time. His jaw dropped in shock. "Dierra, if we want to get the limited-edition Breakdancing Tierra shirt, we have to go now!" he said, his tail flinching madly.

Dierra nodded. "Of course. How could I forget? Do you three wanna get festive too? I know you two would totally *rock* a Tierra haircut. Later — Holly and other two!" They then ran off through the gates, not looking back once.

Birch looked at Alada. "I have a feeling that we won't be sleeping very well tonight." And as if on cue, a stream of firework erupted into the sky, followed by the sound of a roaring crowd.

"Maybe we can still warn them before the party st—" Alada said loudly, in her effort to compensate for the new level of noise.

"Oh my gosh, let's go, LET'S GO! Come on, COME ON!" Tierra squealed with excitement, grabbing them again by the wrists and dragging them in.

Tierra-Meus of all different colors filled the town square with talking, dancing, and firing fireworks. Fog billowed everywhere with neon lights flashing randomly, piercing through the night sky. Alada and Birch walked stiffly behind Tierra, who was weaving them wildly around large groups, shouting out random song lyrics along with dozens of other cats, and showing them her favorite merchants. Birch had to pause several times to shake the excessive confetti and the occasional sticky poster that would cling to his feet and fur. Vendors shouted out deals like:

Two for one for FREE!
One hundred percent off any Tierra merch!
All you can drink smoothies to keep you up all night!
The buildings of wood were shaped like cubes and domes.

Posters of up-coming events plastered the nearby structures.

This is too much, Birch thought. Visions of Central Village—calm, quiet—rose in his mind, and for a moment, he felt a little more grounded. *Way too much.*

"No, it's not," Tierra corrected.

"Huh?!" said Birch, wondering if he had been thinking aloud.

"Huh? Who? What? Where? Geez, what's on your nerves? This place is great! Now, let's get you a Breakdancing Tierra shirt."

"No, no, no, that's not necessary. Jasmine, back me up! All this stuff is insane!"

"Yes," Tierra interrupted. "But we all have a one hundred percent discount on it!"

Alada shrugged uncertainly. "It is a smidge much. Shouldn't we stop 'shopping' and at least get to the Hopper Pop Tierra stop thingy? That would be a good place to talk to a large group of these townsfolk. Do they have a committee? Leaders? Elders?"

Tierra dropped the bag of Tierra treasures she was holding. "You're right, we should just get the shirts and sign-up for the Dance-off," she said, running towards a crowd of Meus that were trying to get their paws on as many different colored Breakdancing Tierra shirts as possible.

"That's not answering her question!" called Birch. Irritation filled his throat and he had to cough. Or maybe it was just a lot of dust … or confetti.

Alada couldn't hide her puzzled expression. "Does she

expect us to follow her or—" She was interrupted by the crowd of Meus arguing ever more loudly amongst themselves as they waited to get the Breakdancing Tierra shirts.

Birch's bulging, unblinking eyes and fluffed tail were clear tells of frazzled nerves. Alada put her hand on his shoulder as he stood quietly amongst the ruckus. "You okay?" she asked.

He slowly nodded.

"Do you want me to step out with you to a quieter place?"

Though unblinking still, he shook his head.

"What do you need right now to help you?"

He shrugged.

"Water? Food?" She looked around at the nearest food vendors who were selling swirled cloud-like candies, midnight salmon… "Would you like some midnight salmon?" she asked him, her hand still on his shoulder.

He nodded half-heartedly.

"Okay, then. Fried or chocolate covered?"

His eyes bulged even more and a sickly expression crossed his face as he stared at her.

"Neither it is," she continued. "I don't see any fruit or vegetables or regular fish stands…" She searched around. "I know you haven't eaten enough, nor rested enough today." Concern swelled in her chest as she watched Birch swaying on the spot. "Sleep. Let's choose sleep first. I guess we have to wait to warn … well, maybe I still can talk some sense into … Let's go find you a place to sleep."

All the unnatural neon lights, loud music, and the sheer

number of Tierra-like Meus — was difficult to adapt to. Birch thought back to his quiet village and remembered the reverence for Tierra. This bright-colored-super-wow, loud and crazy town was everything he had been taught not to indulge in. It just wasn't their way. He sighed uncomfortably. His feet itched to carry him away to another place. Somewhere … quiet.

Birch put down the armfuls of Tierra whatnot and stretched backwards so much that Alada feared he may fall over. "Yeah, I think I will go to sleep. Unlike Holly, I don't want to waste my energy partying all night. I think there's some free lodging over there." He waved his left paw toward a vacant inn.

"Good idea. I'll keep talking to Holly. Good night, Birch" she said.

"Good night, Jasmine," he said – mid-yawn – while turning away. He looked back behind him. "Oh, and thanks." Picking up his traveling bag, he walked over to the inn's entrance and hit his head on the doorway. *"Stupid Tierra -sized doors…."* Alada heard him mutter.

Boom.

Boom.

Boom.

"WHAT IS UP MY PARTY CATS?!"

Alada spun around to see the commotion.

Standing atop a stage with multi-colored spotlights, highlighting her glowing figure, was Tierra. Fully transformed for battle (or as Tierra would say, "A form fit for the spotlights" and "The purest I'll be for my admirers."), Tierra stood center-stage in all her glory — as the real Tierra, not Holly.

Kierra handed her a wooden-looking microphone, and she immediately sang into it.

No, no, no. It's one thing to be in disguise and another to make it widely known that you are here, Alada thought. *We're supposed to be warning them about the Phantom.* Her wings twitched impatiently. She had not flown in days. *I could get this mission done faster if I flew over the forest canopy from town to town.* She reminded herself of her own non-interference clause, annoying as it now seemed to be.

She stood, thinking, amidst the thumps of bass of a particularly thumpy song and dancing Meus nearby. *I doubt we could find elders at this time of night unless we go door to door.*

An elder she-cat with a cane and a sparkly Tierra-styled hairdo hobbled by with a grin on her face.

"Or they'll be partying," she said aloud though no one could hear her. She sighed. "I doubt we'd get anyone to listen to us tonight when we look like –" she looked down at her mortal outfit "–strangers."

Alada thrashed her tail, irritably to the beat. *Can't live in fear, either. They could be attacking another town like ...* her thoughts went to the Pyrite Peaks, her homeland and she felt her heart squeeze. *Or maybe they're not attacking anywhere tonight.*

During her next audible sigh that no one could hear, she

looked up and admired the stars. It was quite late. The elders would either be at tonight's party or in bed asleep.

Still... would strangers from the other villages come in and share immediately? Or would they come and say something in the morning after traveling all day? She took a deep breath to calm down.

Still, Tierra was breaking the rule by showing herself as a Guardian when they hadn't agreed to reveal themselves. *All that matters at this moment is getting her off that stage.* Seconds later, a vision of the Meus attacking her for trying to rip Tierra from the stage came to mind. *Won't win me any trust with that move.*

Tierra's voice echoed into the trees. It was lovely, actually, with a balanced vibrato holding out a perfect note.

Okay. Maybe I don't have to get her off the stage. The right path is not always the obvious one. We can't live in fear, we got in late, Birch is already in bed. She told herself she'd stand watch through the concert.

"Once again kits and kats of all ages," Kierra announced, "Our favorite Tierra the Great has descended upon our stage to delight us with her righteous party spirit!" The crowd roared in support.

Alada felt her ears flatten with her expression. No surprise.

As she looked around the crowd of all ages, she noticed two Meus who stood with nonplussed expressions on their faces, standing fairly close by.

Who are they, I wonder? Uneasiness tugged at her chest.

One of them was a female Meu with an overgrown choppy haircut, and the other was a male wearing a faded Tierra-themed tee. They glanced at Alada, exchanged a look with each other, and motioned her to come over.

Perplexed, Alada pointed to herself. *Me?* she mouthed. Speaking would be no use, even for communicating short distances.

Rolling their eyes, they padded over, pushing their way through the roaring crowd of fans. As they got closer, she realized they were twins.

"Don't tell me you're associated with *her*," the female Meu hissed.

Alada took a step back. "What do you mean?"

"You're a Meu, right?"

"Well—"

"So, do you worship her?"

"No, I do not."

The twins looked mildly pleased. "Do you wanna help us with something?" the male Meu said.

Alada stood silently, not responding.

He continued. "You seem like a cat that can get behind the scenes. We're here to expose her. The whole town's hypnotized. We've got the layout, the tools, and a plan to bring these Meus to a true leader. You in?""

The fur on the back of her neck prickled. She had to force it to stay down. "A *true* leader?"

"A *true* leader," they repeated.

Oh no, Alada thought. *I didn't see an uprising as an issue.*

She scanned the crowd, and sure enough, there were several pairs of similarly bored Meus stationed around the stage — too evenly spaced, too still.

A sense of foreboding settled over her like a heavy fog.

The flashing lights pulsed in and out of focus as she searched for the source of the unease. The music faded into the background as she honed in on a new sound: quiet paw-steps circling the outskirts of town.

Fshhhhhh … stsssss!

Fire?! she thought.

Alada snapped back to the present just as a long stream of flaming fireworks shot up behind the crowd. The Meus from the crowd all turned around momentarily, all except the bored Meus who then scattered into the woods—dropping glass spheres as they ran, which shattered on impact, creating an invisible barrier containing the entire once-cheering group within it.

Tierra's singing faltered when the not-so-invisible barrier began to appear behind the crowd. She stopped all together when the shrieking began.

When the sudden firework show had almost faded from the crisp blackish-blue sky, sparks rained down into the forest — instantly igniting before anyone could react.

Alada stood far enough from the group to see the impact — the entire crowd was now surrounded by an invisible barrier and the once bored Meus reemerged slowly from the woods with dark smiles on their faces. A few Meus coughed. Someone pointed upward — the smoke was getting thicker. Still, no one moved.

Once they had dispersed across the circumference of the circle, they drew their battle staffs (which had little Tierra bobble heads on the tops of all of them. And whenever they hit an opponent, it would make a little "Hiya!" sound.).

Alada stood and watched; she couldn't tell what was going on. *What were they planning?*

Moments later, tendrils of fire began to creep onto the houses and merchant shops. Smoke filled the air, stinging her nose. All the Tierra-Meus turned to their superior, Tierra, wide-eyed with fear and anticipation. They were all thinking the same thing: What was she going to do?

The silence lasted for only a few moments, though, because not even a second later, Dierra grabbed Kierra's megaphone and announced, "OKAY, KITS AND KATS! THE HIP HOP TIERRA POP DANCE-OFF — BATTLE EDITION — IS ABOUT TO COMMENCE! TIERRA THE GREAT — VERSUS — THE TRAITOR MEUS!!!"

The audience cheered in approval. Streams of fireworks exploded into the air and confetti rained down upon them. Someone started up some peppy battle music, then ten air horns went off at once: MEW—MEW-MEW-MEW-*MEEEWWW!*

Air horns, now?? Alada thought. "THE FIRE – these aren't special effects!" she screamed, running up to the nearest Meus. "The fire is REAL!"

"Yeah, REAL AWESOME!" called a Meu who began to hop up and down again.

They all jumped up and down to the music chanting, "HIP, HOP! TE-AIR-RA POP! HIP, HOP! TE-AIR-RA POP!"

Tierra's eyes lit up. She raised her paw and unleashed a flurry of spores, pulled from her confetti bag, which flew over the barrier and rained onto the anti-Tierra Meus. *Wait for it.* The traitors were stunned by the unfazed townsfolk. One after another, the spore-affected traitor-Meus collapsed to the ground. They appeared to be in a dangerously deep sleep.

The Tierra-Meus cheered, and even more air horns sounded off their victory.

Although the immediate threat appeared to be over, the fire raged on. The music, confetti, and all the colored lights, made the Meus oblivious to the fact that everything was truly burning.

At least everyone is safe for now in this cage of invisible force those Meus placed on us, Alada thought. *WAIT. Where's Birch? Right … he's in the inn.*

Chapter 17
The Inn

Birch rubbed his head as he walked into the empty inn. Literally, not a single soul was around. *This place is so vacant — there's not even one spider or mouse.* He walked to the front desk to find himself a key, which was coated in a thick layer of dust and moldy confetti, and it wreaked of decay. Padding carefully behind it, watching out for cracks in the splintered wood, he found a drawer in the back of the desk. Shaking it open, he found a large keyring with about fifty keys. *I have my choice of any room I want.*

Remembering how crummy the inn was — he had second thoughts.

Boom, boom, boom!

"WHAT IS UP MY PARTY CATS?!"

Birch scrunched up his forehead. All he wanted to do was get away from the incessant noise outside. Sadly, the thin, cheap walls didn't help conceal the ruckus. Loud music started playing, and with that, the ground vibrated slightly, and the hanging lights swayed. He frowned, his tail drooping on the floor.

I'll take a room at the back of the top floor, he decided. With that, he carefully walked over to the rotting stairs and slowly ascended as many floors as he could. While many would think walking around in a dark, empty hotel may seem creepy, Birch didn't mind, as he had lived in a ghost town. Ghosts, of course, did not phase him.

The keys didn't work on the farthest room doors, so he found that one closer to the action was all he could do.

"Oof," Birch sighed. The moment he opened the door, a flurry of dust, hair, pollen, and ash flew into his face. He sneezed. The room was about twelve tail lengths by eight tail lengths, and covered in a thick layer of dust. Piles of moth-eaten clothes sat molding on the floor, outdated Tierra-event invitations lay scattered about, and an eerie photo hanging on the wall of when the town was old and the inn was new hung askew.

"And I thought my old home was haunted…"

He padded over to the bed, although it looked more like a wet, moldy, sponge than a comfy thing to sleep on. He patted it firmly.

No dust? he thought.

"Oh." Birch lifted his paw, and it was covered in a thin layer of gray paste. Glancing up, he saw a rusty, cracked copper pipe with water trickling steadily onto the center of the bed. His nose scrunched up. Hesitant to sleep on the finest of smelly dust-paste, he laid a towel from his pack onto the mattress. He awkwardly maneuvered onto his towel, trying to ignore the squeaking of the bed frames and creaking of the splintery floors.

Curled up with his knees to his chin, and tail tickling his nose, Birch tried to fall asleep.

Drip … Drip … Drip.

It was still dark when he woke up light-headed.

Is it just me or is that … Birch thought. *Smoke?*

Birch shrugged and curled up tighter. *Probably just a broken fog machine.*

His vision momentarily blurred as he looked out the dirty windows into the forest and saw what could have been a black hooded figure just outside the window.

"I need some water," he decided, fumbling out of bed towards the bathroom. The bathroom's gray walls sported a faded flowery wallpaper with black mold spots. Glancing over at the sink, he regretted getting up. Next to the sink, there was a greasy cup with fuzzy dust on the edges, and slimy mushrooms filled the sink. It smelled more or less like a smoked, mummified mouse made of decomposing beans.

"Nope," he said as he turned around and left. Suddenly, a wave of nausea overcame him as he started coughing. *Geez, why is there so much smoke?! There was none a minute ago.* His eyes filled with water, his vision becoming blurry. Shrieks sounded from outside. He stumbled over to the window and almost didn't believe what he saw. "No, no, no, *no!*"

Around the town was a ring of fire. All the Tierra-Meus

were surrounded by … other Meus?

Crack — creek — creek sounded above his head.

Someone's on the roof, Birch thought. *I need to get out of here. Now.*

He swung his soggy backpack onto his shoulder and ran for the open door, but made it there too late. The inside of the inn had already been set ablaze. The difference in temperature created a draft so strong it slammed the door shut, thus giving him a face full of Door a la Door.

The window! I can use my double pointed staff to get down the side, or I'll just have to jump.

"Oh, if I were you, I'd go already," a bitter voice said from behind him.

Birch felt his hackles rise and his eyes slitted. How someone got in without him knowing, he wasn't sure.

"I need a high vantage point to observe the oncoming battle… Sadly, you won't be in it," the voice mocked.

Birch spun around just in time to see the hooded figure come out from a veil of smoke and raise its paw towards his face. Under its hood, he saw a pair of glinting yellow eyes, filled with delight, pearly pointed teeth, and black fur.

"The era of Tierra — has fallen." The black cat clenched his paw as Birch frantically ran for the window. Although he only had about two seconds, max, to escape, he might have made it, if not for his exhaustion, which made his legs wobbly.

A loud crack sounded from the floor beneath him, accompanied by the rush of flames. He and everything around him fell into the fiery levels of the inn underneath.

The last thing he remembered before colliding with the flaming floors was the platform above him sealing itself up with melted ash, and burned pieces of wood and tile, in order to make a standing place for the black-hooded cat.

Alada couldn't shake the feeling. It nagged and pulled at her until she sloughed off her backpack and spread her wings. Not one partying Meu even noticed as she rose into the air and sped off to find Birch. She thought he would be more safe away from the party, but the pit of her stomach said the complete opposite now.

Birch, Birch, Birch, Birch, Alada thought as she sped through the air, though she unknowingly held her breath amidst the sight no one else was likely to see – the inn Birch had sauntered into earlier lit the night sky as a raging fire ravaged all floors, all sides, all everything. *Oh my...* she thought, hovering for only a moment over the dancing, clueless crowd. With a great flap of her wings, she rocketed forward and landed before the inn as it burned. Nothing-ness filled her mind as she tried to feel for where he might be among the flames while hopelessness attempted to storm her mind. *Feel... feel, feel!* she shrieked in her own mind, while fluttering about the differing levels. The highest floor, she now noticed, hadn't been fully engulfed yet, and as she began to ascend to the nearest window on the upmost floor, the front wall of the entire inn crumbled and for a split second, noticed a body fall through the floors.

Without thinking, and almost falling to the ground, she landed and burst through the flaming ruins, navigating fiery beams, furniture pieces, and other wooden slabs of flooring, all while aiming for the spot where the body she had seen was likely to have landed. Within fifteen feet in the flames, she found a body and yanked it from the devouring flames. Once outside some forty feet away, far enough to not still feel the scorching heat, she laid his body on the compacted dirt walkway. "Birch!" she whispered, seeing his limp, unconscious body unmoving. "Birch! Birch, please. Please, Birch. Birch!" she now yelled, gently shaking his head and more roughly jostling his shoulders. "Birch, you have to wake up!" her voice cracked.

She looked around for anyone else who could help, but most Meus were at the stage or at home, seeing as how only a couple of homes in the not-so-far distance had lights in the windows.

"Birch!" she called again, tears coming to her eyes. "Please, Birch! WAKE UUUUP!" she screeched, to which he inhaled sharply, coughing incessantly. "Atta boy, atta boy. Wake up. Wake up. Wake up." She didn't help him sit up just yet. "Just breathe."

He tried to lift his head, but it didn't work. She sat there with him, watching around them, should a beast come out of the darkness. Need to move him somewhere safe, she thought, searching around, but nowhere looked safe. Nothing felt safe enough.

"We're under attack," he whispered, trying to get up.

"Yes, but you need to sit this one out. It's not safe for a Mew who feel through… well, however many floors."

"But I didn't die," he said, looking around with a mild alertness. "Got the wind certainly knocked out of me." He barely sat up enough to look around. "I don't see any beasts."

"They're coming, I'm sure of it," Alada said, still hearing the music. "Any minute now."

"We need to save them all," he said, coughing from the smoke while noticing his clothing was well singed and burned in multiple spots. He held his head, dizzy from the smoke.

"I need to save you first," she commanded. He looked into her worried eyes, which were large and tearful. "You're more important than you know." He didn't answer, but she did continue. "We need you. You're the first friend I've had in a…" she choked back a sob, "a really long time." Again, he didn't answer, but did smile, and together, they rose to a standing position. "I still think you should sit this one out," she said. "I will use my true form at this point."

He shot her a look. "What do you mean, your true form? You're not a cat?" He limped and slid back to the ground.

She wanted to smile, but the tension of knowing the beasts could attack at any second stifled the moment. "I'm a Guardian, Birch," she said. "I'm Alada, not Jasmine."

Birch's eyes widened. His mouth opened, but no words

came out. Her large wings immediately caught his attention, granted it was like seeing slight double vision still.
"You really do look like an angel," he said looking from
her wings to her eyes and back again. Suddenly, he looked
away, watching the burning inn. "Woah, that's a big fire,"
he said, his head physically moving slightly as if unable to
balance it.

"I can't stop the fire right now. I have to be ready for
bigger problems."

He nodded. "Are we a safe enough distance?" He fanned
himself. "It's really hot."

"You're safe. We're safe. It's the minimal safest distance
because I needed to bring you to consciousness as fast as
possible. Heat wasn't my number one concern."

He nodded again, steading himself as he tried to stand
once more. "Is Holly a normal cat?"

Alada felt her own face fall and she felt herself pause before answering, feeling unsure how he would react. "She's
Tierra, Guardian of the Bioluminescent Forest."

He stared unblinkingly for a moment. "I need to…"

"Sit down?"

"No, yes, no?" he moved about, rubbing his paws on his
face and about the air strangely. "You're Guardians? Both
of you?"

She nodded.

"And I didn't deserve to know earlier *because*?"

"Because we were trying to stay undercover. One of our
rules is to not let mortals know we're here so they don't rely

on us … or so we don't change their natural evolution."

"Oh, but I'm a mortal who doesn't deserve to know even though we're on the same mission side by side?"

"I didn't mean it that way, Birch," she said, a pleading tone in her voice. "Please, I didn't mean to insult you. I am telling you because I don't think it's a good idea to hide as Jasmine any longer. Our world needs the Guardians now, not Holly and Jasmine."

Birch's eyes teared up as he shifted his feet and weight from one foot to another. "*I* needed Holly and Jasmine."

"We're still here, but it's best you be told first who we are before we tell anyone else. You have become a critical member of our team. I can't imagine doing this mission without you, and I know Tierra feels the same."

"She said that?"

"No, but I can feel it. I know it."

Parts of the inn continued to collapse in bigger and bigger sections, which thundered and spat fire into the air — yet the nearby music raged on. Birch pulled Alada farther away from the collapsing building. "You sure don't seem to fear death," he said. She didn't reply to his remark. "Sorry to pull you out of harm's way, even though you can't get hurt. Just a habit called manners I was once taught."

"Birch," Alada said, "Thank you for your valliant chivalry in so many cases, such as this. Thank you for caring about me and Holly."

"You mean Tierra."

"Yes, Tierra," she said. "I can get hurt. I broke my ribs at the raid in the Central Village. I just ... heal faster." Birch nodded. "You must sit and rest until the attack starts, which may only be seconds away. As your friend, I ask you to sit this one out for your protection and safety. It's harder than you know for a Guardian to watch those they care about die. As a Guardian, I would be honored to have you by my side."

Birch didn't smile, but Alada could feel a calm affection emanate from his gaze. "Me too."

Chapter 18
Tierra's Mistake

Tierra watcched as Alada took off her backpack, spread her wings, and flew over the border.

She squinted toward the woods. Flames licked the sky. A burning tree crashed down behind the crowd. "I can fix trees later," she told herself.

But the knot in her stomach tightened.

Dierra raised her microphone, and the music stopped. "ALL RIGHT, KITS AND KATS! AFTER THAT *LAME* DISPLAY OF MISTRUST, IT'S TIME FOR THE HIP-HOP TIERRA POP DEEE-AAA-NCE OFF — NOR-MAL EDITION — TO COMMENCE!"

The crowd cheered and loud dance music started, and all the Meus danced once more.

Although she loved being with her ultimate fans, her body writhed with the discomfort within her. *What am I doing?* Her dancing faltered slightly. *This is my favorite place, and I'm letting it burn? Wait ... that must be what Alada is doing, trying to stop the flames! Yes, of course .... Still, I probably should evacuate the town.* "Everybody—!" Tierra shouted.

"—IT'S TIME FOR OUR FAVORITE PART OF THE PARTY," Dierra continued excitedly, "GLITTER-BOMB KARAOKE!!!"

Cheers erupted from the cats as hot pink spotlights fell upon Tierra. Kierra rolled a sparkly pillar showcasing a big red button atop with rainbow rhinestones covering the entire thing.

She stood frozen on the spot. All eyes were one her. Everyone was smiling. Everyone was excited. Everyone was waiting … Waiting for her to push the button. Everyone.

She glanced down at a kitten in the front row who looked up at her hopefully.

Maybe the danger is really over? Those weren't beasts. The threat is gone. Traitors and beasts would be a one in a million chance.

The kitten walked up to the front of the stage and placed her paws upon it, still looking at Tierra. "Ti-air-ra!" she chanted, encouragingly.

"Ti-air-ra!" a few others chanted as well.

"TI-AIR-RA! TI-AIR-RA! TI-AIR-RA!" everyone chanted, louder and louder.

There aren't any beasts. Alada's taking care of the fire. I took care of the traitors. It's safe now.

She pushed the button.

A deep, guttural roar split the air. At first, it was almost swallowed by the music, but then came the pounding—pawsteps so heavy they shook the ground beneath the dancers. Glitter burst into the air, shimmering under the stage lights as the Meus danced harder, the beat vibrating through their bones.

Through the haze of fire-smoke and flashing lights, hulking shapes began to materialize—beasts bristling with ropes, chains, and all manner of wicked tools. Their leader pushed to the front, stepping into the glow just behind the crowd, teeth gleaming teeth gleaming like freshly oiled daggers.

It opened its slobbery mouth wide and hollered at the top of its lungs, in an attempt to be heard over the booming music.

"TURN OFF THE MUSIC AND LISTEN TO—"

No one noticed. Dierra and Kierra twirled through their duet, firing a T-shirt cannon in perfect time with the song's climax. The lead beast reeled back, choking on a mouthful of cotton shirts proudly blazoned: #TierraGirl.

"ENOUGH! YOU ARE ALL NOW UNDER THE COMMAND OF THE—"

A glitter cannon exploded point-blank. The crowd roared with delight. Somewhere in the chaos, the title "Rainbow Disco Beast" was born.

"YOU WILL ALL PERISH UNDER–"

The DJ cranked the bass. The beat consumed his threat whole. The music raged on—louder, wilder—until the invasion felt less like an attack and more like the world's strangest afterparty.

"STOP IT!" the leader roared, with segments of its body glitching in and out of existence, scattering glitter everywhere.

"*Cats…*! I *hate* CATS! I just want to destroy them all!" the leader growled to his troops. "FORGET CAPTUR-ING THE MEUS, I JUST WANT THEM ALL DEAD!"

Another beast stumbled backward, yanking a mouthful of t-shirt from his face. He retreated to the side of his first officer.

"Kill them all," growled the leader.

The first officer nodded and motioned with his left hand for an attack. The force-field barrier lifted — now the smoke could permeate the group of partying cats, now the embers could float down onto their whiskers, now the real-ity could come to their senses.

The last air horn sounded and faded into the soft crackles of a fire quietly burning the entire village.

In these few quiet moments, Tierra felt almost discon-nected from her body — as if she could float out of her body in the moment. The embers fell like rain, sporadic cries of fear rang, and all eyes stared at her in expectation.

I haven't needed to fight like this in years, Tierra thought, standing still. She could hear her own breathing amid the crackles of the burning trees and buildings.

The beasts encircled the group once more, bearing arms so large that war-hammers looked like a kitten's toy.

The banners, the t-shirts, the confetti … now mindless chatter of delusion. The Meus, young and old, now scram-bled closer to her as the beasts stepped aggressively forward.

"You'll save us, right?" begged a mother, holding her young child.

Tierra only shifted her eyes downward toward her.

The full regalia of her majesty did not improve nor harm her confidence. She shook her head to release the frozen response from her body and re-entered reality.

They need their Guardian.

The timelessness that followed her enabled a strangely nimble, slow-motion, yet fanatical speed to present itself. The land of no thought, no noise, no feeling, had entered and allowed for only action to preside in the realm of her perspective.

Raising her paws, she summoned a roaring wave of stone and mud that slammed into the beasts with enough force to send them flying twenty feet. For a moment, they were buried — but then, with a jarring shimmer in the air, several of them blinked back to their feet, glitching into their previous positions like shadows snapping back after being momentarily torn away.

Not all of them could glitch at once, though — she noted the slight delay between movements, the shimmer of a recharge window. They were powerful, but not perfect. She could work with that. *Three-second delay. That's all I need.*

Tierra remained in that heightened state where every movement felt both rapid and deliberate, as she walked down the center stage steps, stooped to pick up a Tierra-size staff, and marched toward the first beast she could find.

It couldn't even get up as she wailed on him mercilessly, notwithstanding the "Hiya" sound effects emitting from it until it broke over his head. Yet with her speed and abled-nimbleness, she freely took out every aggression she had ever felt on multiple beasts within a minute.

She moved too quickly, with no warning or rhythm — faster than their glitch reflex. The beasts' glitching, a jerky instant-teleportation normally triggered by danger, lagged behind her attacks. Some tried, their forms warping like heat haze around a flame, but her blows landed before their magic could catch up.

As the second to last beast groaned and fell, save for the leader, cowardly staying in the back, the noise returned; the smells returned, and the truth surfaced.

Chants of "TIERRA! TIERRA!" thundered through the air—then shattered into a stunned, breathless silence. The leader's smile twisted, his form stuttering in and out of reality until, with a final flicker, he was gone. A heartbeat later, the sky ignited—fireballs the size of boulders plummeted into the crowd, shattering on impact and spraying shards, gravel, and choking stone dust in all directions.

"RUUUUNN!" Tierra screamed, hissing a cry so loud that tears poured from her eyes.

The screams and thuds instantly etched in her mind as she tried to use her powers, her staff — anything — to stop them. Yet she couldn't stop even one!

Nothing. Worked.

Boooooooooom.

Booooooom.

Boom.

Booooooooooooooom.

Screams filled the air. Cries of kittens filled the air. Orders from she-cats and tom-cats echoed.

Overwhelmed with grief and rage, Tierra did what she could to help those get out of the way of the falling projectiles.

Crack! Crashhhhhhh.

Mothers and kittens, the elders, warriors, the shop owners. There's just too many, she thought as she calculated the trajectories and dodged amidst the would-be comets.

Even saving the mothers and kittens could hardly save her from herself as she continued to, with her most godly speed, go even faster to save as many as she could.

When she cleared the stage arena of the living, she heard more screaming and watched as the flaming boulders flew into the village, into the forest … relentlessly.

Entering the residential lanes, she watched helplessly. Even as a goddess, Tierra didn't have the power to stop the endless rain of flaming boulders. All she could do was to try to help all the Meus that were frantically trying to escape their homes as they caught fire.

As she approached one home with a mother and five kittens, she saw a boulder falling straight for it. Without thinking, she bounded off the sides of the other homes and pawed the flaming mass from the side, throwing it off course, smashing it into a giant tree. Overcoming all of the endless boulders was useless, as there were too many, going in too many directions, to push out of the way, and her charred hands seared with pain.

She knelt to the ground as the cries and fire continued

to rain down. Tears poured from her eyes. "I can't do this anymore! I can't do this alone!" she shrieked. *What kind of goddess am I? … a pathetic one.*

She didn't know how long she had been kneeling, but an odd sound attracted her attention. The boulders had stopped hitting the village. A chill ran down her spine … *If not being aimed here …, where did they go?*

Birch whizzed by, escorting some other male Meus with weaponry out of the village.

"Get up, Tierra!" he hissed. "Get up!" Birch's angry eyes held little compassion or fear. "This is no time for emotional self-pity! Get up!"

She instantly stood, and as she did so, noticed movement in the corner of her eyes. Alada, in her full regalia of a flowing white and blue gown with golden armor, flew quietly overhead, incinerating the boulders on contact.

"MOVE!" Birch ordered, as he then firmly commanded the other males on their expectations for protecting the she-cats and kittens.

Tierra *did* move. Somehow, knowing Birch and Alada didn't abandon her — in all honesty, she had forgotten them entirely — helped her feel rejuvenated and strong. She picked up her staff and trotted off to catch whoever was procuring the fireballs.

"I know where you're going," Alada called down from her heavenly, most etheric position in the sky. "But you won't find whoever started it. The fireballs have stopped."

"Ground patrol," Tierra called. "Have to secure the perimeter."

Alada landed with a quick, but graceful thud. "Securing the perimeter should have been FIRST. These Meus have nowhere to live now."

The silence between them was deafening.

Something could have been said, a warning could have been given, a party didn't have to happen … something could have been done. They could have protected themselves. They could have evacuated, thought Tierra.

"I trust I don't have to say more," Alada remarked angrily. She marched off, attending to the cries of mothers and kittens and those of the injured.

Shame and guilt washed over Tierra like the most unwelcome, sour, despicable bath she had ever experienced. Everybody that now lay still as she passed, every mournful cry of a loved one, every burnt home — was because of her … and she *knew* it.

Holding such a level of grief was not possible as she soon vomited into the bushes. The crowd had once chanted her name. Now, not even the trees echoed it back.

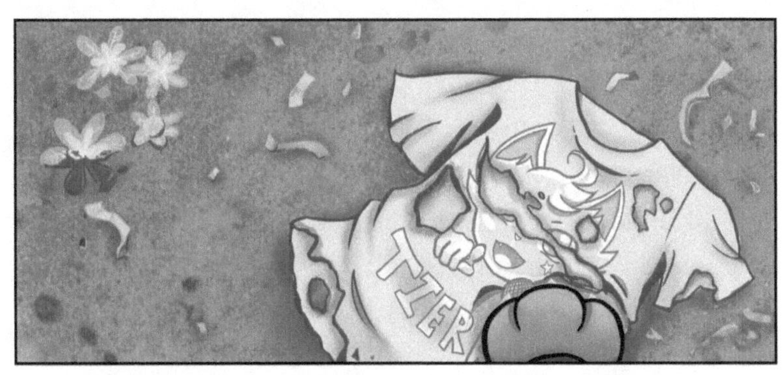

Chapter 19
The Reckoning

How can your beasts be so stupid?!" the Phantom hissed menacingly at the general. "Those brain-dead mutts can't even glitch. I gave them power and they can't seem to do the easiest of things. *Use it.*" The Phantom paced circles around the tall beast, leaving an icy draft in his wake.

The tall, black cat smirked at the general, tiny blue flames dancing in his paws.

Turning its head, the Phantom glared at him, its cold black eyes like daggers.

"Smack that smile off your face, *Kitty.* There's still something I need to talk to you about."

"Don't refer to me as *Kitty,*" the black cat growled.

"Okay then, *Toasty Mittens,*" the Phantom mocked. The cat scowled, but said nothing. The Phantom, pleased to have silenced him, continued to speak, "You did an *acceptable* job in the village, better than last time."

"I do what I can—"

"According to the general, though, it appears you stopped

attacking halfway through."

"I already destroyed everything. Why waste more energy? Especially with those two goddesses there."

The Phantom narrowed its eyes. "You told me you knew how to deal with them. I can't afford false information," the Phantom threatened. Holding eye contact for a moment longer, the cat lowered his head and grinned widely.

"Don't worry, I know their ways. The time just hasn't come yet."

The smoke had thinned, but the sting still hung in the air. Soot coated the grass, the fur of the Meus, and the charred remains of what had once been homes. A crowd had formed in the clearing amongst the rubble — silent at first. Then, one voice broke through.

"You knew, didn't you?"

Tierra turned, her soot-streaked face unreadable.

"You came with the others to warn us," said a gray-furred elderly Meu, stepping forward with a shaking paw, "but you danced instead. You joined the festival. You said nothing."

The silence deepened. A few murmurs stirred the crowd.

A younger Meu added, "You smiled. *You smiled,* Goddess Tierra. While our homes were in danger."

Tierra swallowed hard. "I didn't think they'd come so soon—"

"But they did," snapped another, eyes shining with fury. "And now my brother's missing. My aunt—gone. We were laughing while the enemy crept closer!"

A kitten clung to its mother's leg. "She didn't mean it," the child whispered.

"She's a Guardian," the mother replied softly, but not kindly. "She was supposed to guard."

Tierra stood still. She didn't defend herself. Her eyes were low, her tail motionless.

"You failed us," someone said.

"She stayed and fought," replied a very ash-covered Dierra — softer, but firm.

"She fought off the beasts. Not one of us had to fight them or the traitors!" said a younger Meu with broken glasses.

"She can't help fire balls," Dierra said.

"She could have warned us, knowledge notwithstanding," a rather robust male said. "I'm lucky I still have my family, unlike others."

A strong male named Ash stepped forward at last, raising one paw. "Enough," he growled. "She could've run. She could've let us all burn. But she didn't. We're alive because she stayed and bled with us."

The crowd was quiet again.

"I dare say that telling us the moment she arrived would have done nothing against fireballs," Ash said firmly. "She'd have needed to find the elders, gather us all, and even then, the attack came before we could've acted. She immediately stopped the party and took care of danger as it presented itself."

"We still could have fled! Most of us could have made it out," hissed a mother holding her two kittens.

"I understand your anger, but these are assumptions," Ash continued.

"Stop defending her!" cried another younger male. "She knew better!"

"I'm not defending, but Meus do not punish without facts. Assumptions are not facts. Here, there – someone grab Elder Root."

They all turned and saw an elderly Meu sitting calmly on a stump with his Tierra hairstyling still in place due to the extra firm styling gel (made from the gelatin of the milk mushroom) most Tierra Town folk used.

Several Meus padded over and helped half-carry the elder into the ever-growing group. Ash calmly explained the circumstance as Tierra continued to stand silently. The elder nodded with quiet Mm-hmms every so often.

"So?" called voices from the audience.

Elder Root stood, assisted by Ash. "Had she come to us, we wouldn't have met last night. Not until sunrise. We're old, after all. And cautious. And slower to act."

He looked around at the ruin.

"But the fire came faster than sunrise."

Tierra finally stood forward. "Still… I should have tried. I gambled with your peace, and you paid the price. I was wrong." She raised her head. "I deserve your anger," she said simply. "I didn't act fast enough. I thought I could spare you the fear. That was wrong."

A pause.

Then she turned and walked toward the ashes, alone, and began to clear rubble with her bare paws.

Chapter 20
Divided Duties

The town had indeed burnt to the ground. Most of the Tierra-Meus who Tierra passed did not greet her with a smile, but mostly, averted their eyes to another direction.

Alada, on the other hand, was greeted with great generosity and kindness. The townsfolk profusely thanked her for saving them from the fireballs.

"You're welcome," Alada said with a gentle smile.

On the other side of town, Tierra continued to experience something less pleasant, though warranted in her own eyes.

"Have you seen my dad? He looks like you, but not," asked a small kitten, pulling on Tierra's leg.

Tierra's throat tightened, as she was clueless. "I don't know, little one," was all the reply she could muster.

"You did this," came a familiar voice. Tierra looked around and saw Birch scowling at her. "You knew this was a possibility; we came here to warn them," he scorned, quietly, as to not upset the villagers even more. He was so angry tears flowed down his cheeks. "And yet you danced. And yet you sang. And yet you played."

Tierra opened her mouth to speak, tears in her eyes as well, but no words came out. She even tried to mouth words, but nothing was there to mouth. No words could validate what happened or make it right.

By late afternoon the next day, Alada looked around for Tierra, who clearly was nowhere around. "We need to move on, Birch, and warn the other communities. We can assign a couple of the males to warn the smaller villages nearby, but we can't spare more days to help these folks rebuild. They'll have to do that on their own." She fidgeted. "Our continuing to stay could compromise the lives of others."

Birch nodded slowly, though he made no eye contact. He picked back up the wood he had put down and sauntered off toward an open section under the tree's protection. Townsfolk had gathered and were working together to build larger makeshift dwellings for multiple families and other Meus to inhabit until complete reconstruction occurred. He put the wood down by the communal bonfire and a smaller cooking fire.

"A little more to the right, Tierra," called a masculine voice. "A little more."

Birch quickly walked away from the small encampment, which was nestled within a ring of clustered boulders, and spotted Tierra standing a short distance off. Her tail flicked with focus as she extended both paws toward the ground, eyes closed and brow slightly furrowed.

A soft hum filled the air, low and resonant, as if the very stones beneath her were holding their breath.

The framework of a small, one-family shelter — a woven skeleton of roots, vines, and braced wood — sat ready in front of her. With a gentle motion of her paws, the soil beneath it trembled, then obeyed.

From all around, the earth began to shift and rise, like dough stretching toward its mold. Thick panels of compacted soil slid up in slow arcs, curling over the framework like protective arms. Tendrils of moss sprouted instantly along the base, anchoring the walls. The scent of fresh earth filled the air as pebbles clicked into place and ridges formed, grain by grain, smoothing into sturdy walls with delicate leaf-etched patterns across their surface.

Tierra opened one eye to check the symmetry. "You're not allowed to be lopsided," she muttered to the wall, giving a corrective twitch of her paw. The roof adjusted slightly, bending like a polite nod.

Birch stopped mid-step, mesmerized. She wasn't just moving dirt. She was speaking a language he couldn't hear — and the land answered like an old friend eager to help.

As the final layer of earth sealed itself around the structure, a sprout burst from the roof and bloomed in a single breath, releasing a faint shimmer of golden pollen.

Tierra exhaled, then stretched her arms above her head. "One down. Fifty-something to go," she said with a sigh

— though there was a quiet pride in her voice she didn't bother to hide.

"What's going on?" Birch asked, surprised to hear his own voice as he had not intended to interrupt.

"Tierra had a great idea," said the male Meu, hopping down from a boulder.

"Birch, this is Ash. Ash, this is Birch," Tierra called out.

Birch and Ash both nodded at one another.

"Earthen structures," Ash continued, "Fireproof. Easily hidden and unnoticed. Much different from the wooden buildings with florescent neon murals and graffiti." He then walked over to show Birch the newly built structure. "One down," he said. "Based on what Tierra was saying about these beasts, this may be a good way to protect ourselves moving forward. The threat may not be over if this Phantom is trying to take over the other lands and communities. Oh!" he scampered over to the doorway, "And we can hide the entrances, and look!" The Meu covered the entrance with a thick layer of earthen sod and clover. "Blends right in! This is superior to what we had. We can now be safe from any threat."

"Not all will be in mound shapes or it will give them all away," Tierra stated, now standing nearby, building a new mound. "This one will be a decoy." She was sweaty and rather mangey looking, yet she silently worked unless otherwise commanding the next steps of the build.

"Nice," Birch commented, observing the natural curves of each structure. "Reminds me of the Central Village.

Nothing like returning to the basics of natural building."

The other Meu, nor Tierra, remarked but kept working.

"Holly — I mean, Tierra," Birch said. He coughed uncomfortably. "I, uh, need to speak with you."

She merely glanced at the other Meus, stopped working, jumped down from the dome she had created, and walked past Birch onto a narrow forest pathway. When they were far from the others, she turned and stared. "What?" she asked with a somewhat irritable tone.

This offset Birch's emotions, setting him to a feeling of imbalance on his feet. "We should leave to warn the other villages and communities. Alada mentioned something about the Fake Gold Peaks."

Her ear twitched.

"You mean *Pyrite* Peaks?" she asked.

Birch's eyes shifted. "Yeah, that place." He shuffled his feet. "We don't have time to help them rebuild everything at the expense of the other villages," he continued.

"*You* don't have time," Tierra said. "Go ahead without me. I'm staying. Staying to rebuild homes. To rebuild lives. To rebuild... myself."

He shifted his feet.

"Go on, you'll be fine without me. Besides, other than the Bioluminescent Forest, I never liked other territories as much anyway."

"Of course ... Tierra." He had always thought of Holly only as a Meu with a lot of talent, and a portable blender, but now that Holly was Tierra, his perspective on his memories were a lot different. Why did she and Alada not save the first town that was raided by the beasts? Of course, she knew her way through the Lost Labyrinth. Why had he not realized her goddesshood sooner?

Tierra noticed his distress and patted his shoulder. "I'm sorry for not telling you sooner, but tell me, if you knew all along, would you have come with us to warn the villages? No, like most other Meus, you would have trusted us to warn the villages ourselves."

Birch wanted to think that Tierra was wrong, but she was pretty on-point. If he didn't feel the need to leave and alert everyone of the oncoming danger, because someone more capable was doing it for him, then he would have just stayed and helped with repairs in the Central Village like everyone else.

He sighed. "Yeah, you're right," he said, combing his paw through his hair.

Tierra nodded. "Of course I am." She paused. "Don't worry, I'm just teasing you. But now, in all seriousness, I need to get back to work." She gave him a quick side-hug. "See you later — and *don't die*. Alada would probably feel guilty for the rest of her life if that happened."

Birch smiled. "I wouldn't appreciate dying either." He stood there a moment longer and watched as Tierra scampered back to work, his heart twitching slightly as she disappeared. With a deep breath, he turned around and searched for Alada, whom he found watching over some kittens while their mothers hung clothes to dry on a nearby rope line.

"You have everything?" Alada said upon his approach out of the old growth.

"I think so."

"Heavy sweater, fuzzy hat, boots?"

"Yup! Some folks let me have them since I wasn't prepared for snow. I'll go grab my bag. It's close by." He went and returned quickly.

"Now, how long do you think the walk is going to be?" he asked as she rose from her seat, patted the kittens on the head, handed out hugs, and picked up her small satchel.

Before Alada could answer, a mother holding a soot-covered sweater to her chest called out, "Thank you, Goddess Alada. We are so grateful for your motherly spirit toward our kittens."

Another mother Meu chimed in, "Yes, honestly. I believe we shall rewrite the stories to reflect the motherly nature and compassion that has gone unpraised for too long."

Alada smiled and waved to the mothers who called out their gratitude as they turned toward one another and continued discussing how strange it was that this aspect of Goddess Alada had never been known.

"Well, Tierra was the Guardian of the Bioluminescent Forest, so we naturally don't have too many stories of Goddess Alada," chimed in a third mother, who draped a sheet over the rope, accidentally letting the edges fall into the dirt.

"I think we've missed out with only worshiping Tierra.

Maybe we should request of the Creator to allow us to call upon any god or goddess we want as a Guardian," said a fourth mother, who quickly darted after one of the kittens sneaking a berryleaf fruit from her satchel. "That's for after supper!"

Alada hadn't moved, as tears had glossed over her vision. She felt her heart cringe — not out of anger at Tierra, but a deep, familiar softness. A kind of ache that didn't sting with blame, but with memory.

She blinked hard. *Not now.*

Birch coughed, letting her know he was still there. She glanced over, giving a quick nod. "Together, it'll be a week's trek. I already instructed three others to warn the smaller towns nearby."

He bobbed his head, silently pondering the implications of walking for a whole week … Together they silently sauntered toward the exit of the village, purposely not drawing attention to themselves — hoping to slip out of view and not disturb the new foundation the villagers were rebuilding as a community and town.

Still, Birch, being Birch, couldn't help but break the silence. "Maybe I could get on your back and you can just fly us there!" He liked this idea; he always thought it would be cool to fly over the clouds.

Alada's glaring face said it all: No, no, what kind of idea is that, and no.

"Um, I think it would be best if we just picked up a Levi Lift at the border," she said politely, yet spoken in a way that clearly indicated that she was up for no other option.

"Okay," said Birch, wondering what she meant.

At the edge of Tierra Town, all the Meus in view of their departure called out and waved. Alada couldn't help but feel glad to be moving on, but Birch's mixed feelings of leaving without Tierra gnawed at him.

They were the trio. The three-cat squad. The would-be heroes.

Friends.

It felt … emptier.

They waved at those who wished them farewell and trod out of view.

They walked in silence for a little while before Alada spoke again. "Do you know what a Levi Lift *is?*"

"Nope." He picked a leaf off a bush as he walked past. He observed it and began to gently pick it into pieces with each step.

"Well, the easiest way to explain it is two magnets opposing each other. If you angle them right, you can make them float—or *levitate,* you know? The Nyas built these underground transportation devices all over — not too far over the other territories, though."

Birch's eyes had glazed over in confusion. "I think I get it. Underground whatnot. Got it."

She merely smirked as she gently led the way at a pace easier for Birch to maintain over a longer distance. She didn't mind the silence. In fact, she enjoyed it. And honestly, encouraged it.

Birch, however, clearly didn't do well with long lengths of silence and quickly filled it. "Do you think Tierra will join us again?"

She simply shrugged. "Probably. At some point."

"She'll never be the same."

Her ear twitched. "What makes you say that?" She looked at him with a soft gaze in her eyes.

"She was completely different when I talked with her before we left."

"Well," she said, smiling, "Perhaps. Or perhaps we're going to see the true Tierra for once. Perhaps, just perhaps, the all-party-all-the-time … was an aspect not true to her character."

Birch didn't know what to make of it, so he changed the subject. "So, a week's walk, huh?"

She merely nodded, gently purring to herself.

"Twenty-five homes have been built, twelve faux mounds adorn twelve underground structures as both escape routes and traps," said Ash. He had been working all day. His fur was matted with dirt and dust puffed off him with every movement.

"Excellent," Tierra stated. Her new dwelling, a makeshift tent amongst a dirt wall, was lit with lamps both day and night. She stooped over a parchment map on a dirty rug overlaying the dirt floor. "Now, the newly cleared small crop fields should go to the east, near the year-round creek, for irrigation."

"I know you're thinking of building the last of the homes on the edge of the forest, but with the creek so close, the floodwaters may be an issue come winter." He really was a gentle Meu despite his gruff appearance.

Tierra had not looked up to notice the soft gaze he gave her.

"Good point." She hissed to herself. "Push it back into the forest more. Better cover and protection anyway. Fell only dead trees and living trees only absolutely necessary for building materials. Leave as many trees as possible, their root systems strengthen the foundations of the dwellings."

He nodded, but again she didn't notice.

"It's quite the new Tierra Town."

She hissed again, near soundlessly. "You may want to think of renaming it to something more befitting a peaceful settlement."

"You're not going into that again, are you?" he asked loudly.

For once, she looked up.

"The town has already acquitted you of guilt for the attack."

She hissed, her ears flattened, as she gazed back at the paper.

"Yes, I know you said you could have warned us sooner," he said. She looked up sharply. "And didn't," he added. "But you still fought hard to protect us as the godly feline you are." He paused, watching her return to the map. "That's what counts."

His kind words trailed off, but she merely piped in again with "change the name."

"To what?"

She shrugged.

"Shrugville. Peculiar name. I don't think it'll garner much respect," retorted the Meu.

With her pupils mere slits and her tail poofed — he dared not remark anymore.

"I'll, uh, get back to managing the encampment," he said, leaving as he spoke.

"Thank you, Ash." She sat alone, observing her papers. "Seven days," she mumbled. "Seven days and the town basics are already rebuilt. Not bad…"

Chapter 21

The Pyrite Peaks

You want me to what?" Birch asked as Alada sat quietly, expectantly, in a cylindrical half-tube they had located in a dark cave. "Who knows how many eons old that thing is?! It's in this dark cave in the middle of nowhere and you expect me to climb inside?"

After days of walking, Alada was surprised that he was putting up a stink about getting inside. She merely stared at him. "The main community rests in the mountains. I will take the express route at this point, but you may walk, if you see fit. I have no preference on your choice in the matter, but please be aware we are only staying long enough to rest for the next leg."

She continued to stare at his face in the lamplight. "In or out? I'll tell you more on the way. We'll be there in a few hours by use of these levitation rails." She fiddled with the controls, not actually pushing them yet. "You're lucky I remembered this one. I thought it would be another day or two before we'd reach the lowest rail system."

She placed her paw on a small, glowing tablet. The moment she made contact, the top of the tube lit to reveal several active buttons.

Birch clamored in behind her, clearly reluctantly, as he mumbled and fumbled into a seated position. The tube closed itself and sealed seamlessly as if no door had been available. Without a moment's notice, it began to move along effortlessly.

"Good choice," Alada said.

"So, I thought it would be less than a week's trek if we used the lifts and a full week's trek if we didn't use the lifts," Birch said.

"It's a week's trek if we use the lifts. That's what I meant," she said.

"So, if I didn't get in…"

"You'd have several more days to walk … uphill. In the rain. Both ways." She smiled. "Now," Alada began, "These cats are not the same as Meus in the Bioluminescent Forest. These are Nyas. They are proud, strong, and very advanced."

Birch stared with an exaggerated flat expression. "Compared to the Meus who are … unadvanced?"

She coughed, not wanting to mention that "unadvanced" wasn't really a word. "I meant no disrespect, truly," she managed to say. "But it is a very different society, as you will come to understand, of each. The Aras and the Mizus are also very different. All four of the territories have their own social structures, customs, etiquette, and whatnot. Right now, you are stepping out of your own culture and into the land of the Nyas, who strongly uphold honor and respect toward others and self."

"Why've I not heard much of them till now?" Birch said, trying to piece together what little he remembered learning of the mountain race of cats.

"Well, you Meus, are like a tightly knit family. You always stick together and work hard together." She held up her paws. "Nothing wrong with that. Again, I mean no offense in what I'm trying to convey here. But there is a lot more to Felina than you know. You have to understand, you are now in the position as a diplomatic representative of all Meus."

He stared, unblinking. Instinctively, he looked down at his somewhat dirty traveling clothes.

"I'm sure you never expected being in such a position, but there you have it. You are accompanying the Guardians and are out of your territory; therefore, you must understand that all of your words and actions will be judged by the Nyas as words and actions on behalf of all Meus."

Birch placed his paws on the window, but quickly withdrew them. The glass was as cold as a river in the middle of winter. "Every Territory has a god or goddess, right? And if I'm correct, you'd be the Nya's goddess. If so, why were you in the Bioluminescent Forest helping us with things?"

"Helping people makes me happy. I love all within Felina. And besides," she glanced out the window into the dark nothingness, "I was starting to get lonely by myself."

He searched his pockets for anything he could fidget with. "Is it like — a god-law, that you can't visit each other?"

"Yes, and no. No, in that we are not *supposed* to see each other." Alada smiled.

Birch just sat there wide-eyed. "How long ago was that rule made exactly?"

"Maybe a thousand years ago. Wait. How old are you?"

"Twenty-six."

"Oh, I thought you were like nineteen or something. I'm about two thousand-thirty."

"Really? Wow, are you all that old, or did you become immortal at different times? Or … were you always that way?"

"Well, the other Guardians don't like admitting it, but they have been around for a long time too. I'm the oldest at about two thousand-thirty, Ember second at two thousand-twenty, Tierra third at one thousand-eighty, and lastly, Coral at the age of one thousand-forty."

Birch smiled but was a tad confused. "Why are you so open in telling me all of this more personal stuff about you and the others? Like your ages?"

"This is my way of teasing them. Don't tell them I told you this, but *I* actually named the different races. Coral was determined to rename her cats Fursh."

"Fursh?"

"Furry Fish."

"Oh, jeez. "This is changing how I see all of you. What about the others?" he asked, hungry for more godly bloopers.

Alada purred. "If I can recall, Tierra actually wanted to rename your kind: Ti-catz — with a Z. And Ember, in a particularly annoyed state with his subjects, wanted to rename them: The Nuisances with Fur. Nurfs, for short."

Birch had to ponder all this, make sense of these other names. The thought of being a Ti-catz made his head spin. He finally spoke, hesitantly.

"Hey… why did you name everything the way you did? The territories. The people. Does it mean something?"

Alada didn't answer at first. Her gaze lingered on the sky, where dusk met the curve of the land in a perfect hush. Then she inhaled deeply, her voice soft but steady.

"It wasn't really a decision," she said. "It was more… received."

Birch tilted his head. "Received? From who?"

"From the Source," she replied, her eyes far off. "Not like a voice in my head or words etched in fire. More like… resonance. Like tuning a string until it hums just right. Each name wasn't made. It was found."

Birch blinked. "You found the name 'Meus'? Just lying around?"

Alada smiled faintly. "I listened. To what the forest whispered. To what their paws and laughter and song were already saying. Meu is the sound of joy in stillness. Ara is the breath between grief and grace. Nya…" She paused. "That one came in a dream. I woke up weeping and didn't know why. It fit, like the name had always been waiting for them to arrive."

Birch scratched the back of his neck. "That's… heavy. I guess I thought you just liked the sound of it."

"I do. Because it was right." She looked at him now, eyes glowing with something both ancient and utterly present. "Names carry weight, Birch. Especially the ones we speak first. They become prayers—whether we mean them to or not."

Birch looked down the hill at the lands stretching below. Names he had spoken his whole life. Places he'd taken for granted.

And for the first time, he said them quietly to himself—not as geography, but as blessing.

Birch was just about to say something else when a bright white light appeared in the distance.

"I think we're here!" she exclaimed.

His eyes dilated as they came out of the dark tunnel and emerged into a vast, snowy landscape, sparkling like crystals in the shining rays of the sun. Birch, in fact, had never known snow, for the thick canopy of the Bioluminescent Forest never allowed anything other than rain and sometimes light from above. The trees, like none he had ever seen before, were tall and pointed with sparkling white tips. As they raced onward, he saw a large ridge of mountains, the Pyrite Peaks, rising on the horizon. Wisps of cloud drifted across a pale blue sky. The midday sun cast a brilliance Birch had never known.

"I could get used to this," he murmured to himself as a fine layer of snow gently fell around the moving capsule.

Alada smiled, allowing him to take in the moment while she fluttered her snow-white wings.

When the base of the mountain was almost upon them, their Levi Lift slowed down. They arrived at a small, enclosed station with a tiny crowd of five to ten Nyas standing by. Marvelous murals of the Pyrite Peaks, Goddess Alada, and mountains full of trees adorned the walls.

"Okay, Birch, it's time to stop staring. We have to get out," Alada said, opening the capsule door and emerging both quietly and effortlessly.

Birch glanced at her while getting his stuff together and noticed that she had changed back into her mortal form and dress, though with thicker fur.

"Why–?" He wanted to know why she bothered to look mortal at this point.

"I don't want to draw unnecessary attention to myself," she said, discomfort in her tone.

Birch offered his paw to help her out, which she kindly took. He only had a moment to take in the group of Nyas before they filed into the empty seats.

The mountain cats came in shades of white and gray, most with piercing blue or silver eyes. It was easy to see their eye color as each stared at him, wide-eyed and unblinking as they passed. They were fit, almost muscular looking, all with thick, long fur, as Alada's had become. Each of them was half a head taller than he was—or more.

The trek up the rest of the mountain to the Nyas' home base was steep and Birch could hear Alada breathing louder and louder. They stopped for a moment's rest where Birch, wheezing on his own, couldn't help but smile that Alada had reached a point of needing to breathe in an open-mouthed fashion as well.

"Yes, yes," she said, smiling as he turned around to face her, grinning. "My lungs have not been so equipped for steep walking at this altitude, as my wings have always preferred a different approach to the Nya homelands."

Birch said nothing and they were off again with Alada now leading the way.

"Halt!" called a deep, mellow voice. A Nya stood tall and quiet just to the side of the footpath ahead. Clearly, he wasn't going to ask the obvious "Why are you here?" as it was clear it was their turn to speak.

"We—" began Birch, but the Nya saw Alada's wings, now visible, and immediately took a knee, bowing. Birch startled. "Oh, right," he mumbled. "I'm still getting used to all this."

"We come with warning," Alada said, stepping forward.

The Nya stood, stared a second longer, and turned on his heel, leading them along the well-trodden footpath. Silently, they followed. Birch contemplated how long this trek would be when the forest line abruptly stopped and gave way to an expansive, somewhat barren mountain-top.

"Your highness," the Nya spoke, "I can take you to the council unless you have other requirements and needs first."

"Thank you," Alada spoke, "This Meu is named Birch. He and I both would do well with some water, and then would eagerly encourage a meeting with your high council. And say, what is your name, noble guard?"

The Nya stood a little taller. "Sir Carnelian," he stated.

"Very good. Thank you," Alada said, holding out her hand to encourage movement.

As Carnelian led the way, he mentioned to the first Nya he came across to fetch water for "Goddess Alada and her peasant friend."

"Peasant?" Birch mumbled from the far back.

Alada quickly glanced back with a warning in her eyes: Don't get worked up.

More and more Nyas came into view as they walked farther away from the forest and neared the sparse village buildings made of mud brick and stone.

"Is this where they live?" Birch whisper-shouted out to Alada, observing the somewhat impressively sculpted structures before him.

Alada didn't answer but continued gently greeting the Nyas she came upon. Each Nya stood tall but quiet as they all passed, and a large, dark hole in the side of the mountain soon presented itself.

"And you vouch for this — Meu," said Carnelian, cautiously eyeing Birch up and down.

"I do," Alada spoke confidently.

Birch shifted his feet, frowning at the dark hole carved into the mountain.

Carnelian did nothing more but lead the way into the mountain itself. Birch hesitated but forced himself to follow suit the moment he realized Alada wasn't watching to ensure he was following. "Coming! Don't go without me."

They walked through a rather wide corridor until all at once the earth opened up to reveal a vast, deep system of larger tunnels and rooms.

"This is the Nya network," Alada said, turning to Birch. "They live mostly underground — it shields them from predators and the cold. There are dwellings above as well, but primarily the entire community will be found here."

"Under the circumstances," Birch said, "this is an excellent idea."

"Their army is one of, if not *the*, strongest of Felina," Alada spoke.

"I've never heard of their army," he said.

"Great power does not need to show off," she added, simply.

"Do you think they would fight against the Phantom?"

"I'll say no more," she said, now falling entirely silent as Carnelian continued onward into the second tunnel to the right.

Amidst the mazes of corridors and rooms, Carnelian opened an extra-wide stone door and motioned for them to enter. The large room showcased vaulted ceilings and in the center of the space was a circle of many chairs.

Alada took a large chair behind the circle and sat. "You may sit over there," she said to Birch, motioning to a series of chairs lining the east wall.

Birch did as he was told and sat quietly. A Nya entered with waters and silently passed them to both Birch and Alada, who thanked the beautiful Nya respectfully.

After about twenty minutes of waiting, the door cracked open.

Chapter 22
The Council Meeting

Y ou're leaving already?"

"Yes, it is time for me to rejoin my group," Tierra said firmly, while packing water, seeds, split-seed bread, and spiced nuts.

"But this is the first time we've ever had to get to know you," Ash said.

"All you ever need to know is that I'm here to help and protect. That's my job. That's all it is," Tierra remarked with a flat tone.

"Bitter much?"

Silence.

"I will leave you in charge to ensure the plans are completed," she went on.

Ash stopped her mid-packing by taking hold of her shoulders to force eye contact. "Please," he said. "I don't want you to go."

Tierra merely set her eyes, which had glazed over, in his general direction. "We are not the same," she mewed. "You can afford to set your sights on one special Meu, have a family, build a life, and die old in your bed after a life well-lived." She pulled herself from his grasp. "My role is different." She continued to pack at a more hurried pace. "Ensure the changes are met, so that when I return, whenever that may be, you will all be alive and well, safe in well-constructed homes. I cannot assure that the road ahead will be smooth for either of us."

Ash sighed. "Tierra Town will be here."

She cringed at the name but said nothing. Soon after she packed the last bit of food, she hoisted the bag on her back and hurriedly trekked toward the town's exit.

While she had hoped to sneak out of town unnoticed, she turned to look back one last time, and saw a great portion of the town standing silently at the new entrance. One younger Meu held her paw high and blasted off the famous Tierra-Fun air horn: *MEEEEW—MEW-MEW-MEW—MEEEEW!*

But it meant something else now.

They all quietly smiled, allowing her to leave in peace.

Tierra nodded, blinking back the sting in her eyes. She then turned toward the ancient tree just beyond the gate. She lifted a single paw and placed it on the bark. The tree pulsed faintly in response, a soft glow threading through its rings like breath.

Without hesitation, she stepped forward, vanishing into the trunk with the grace of falling light — no sap, no resistance. Just a seamless merging with the forest that had always been hers.

Chapter 22

"Welcome," said Alada as she stood to greet the Nya council as they entered the room. Their eyes grew wide and their hushed whispers were hardly quiet.

"I can't believe she's here," one said.

"What could this mean?" said another.

"A problem, likely," groaned an older Nya.

"Please sit," Alada requested, taking her seat. "It is urgent business."

The Nyas all sat and waited quietly, staring all the while.

"An invasion of so-called beasts has permeated the Bioluminescent Forest under the command of one called the Phantom," Alada stated. "There is viable evidence to conclude the expansion efforts of said Phantom will continue toward the Nya homelands and beyond. We are venturing out to ensure all communities, establishments, settlements, and territories are well-informed of the impending dangers."

Silence prevailed momentarily before a Nya shifted in his chair. "Well," he stated, "We have not noticed any of this so-called evidence, your highness. Though I hardly believe any Phantom could be so powerful as to dare their fate against the Nya homelands."

"The Pyrite Peaks are the strongest of the territories, yes," Alada said, "But do not let a sense of security and authority blind you to the possibility of invasions from what is not a weak enemy. Arrogance never ends well."

"What has occurred in the forest exactly?" another Elder

asked.

She relayed the events in a firm manner.

"There is no telling yet as to how large an army this Phantom may possess," she remarked. "We need more intel."

"Couldn't you fly over? Call upon the other gods if this is such an important threat?"

"Yes, indeed," spoke the more irritable council member, "If this is so serious, where are the other—"

The doors to the council room burst open by the firm push of Carnelian, revealing Tierra standing centered in the doorway, afresh with clean goddess attire.

Gasps around the council echoed in the room as Alada sat, unstirring, from her seat.

Tierra simply stared at the wide-eyed Nyas with unimpressed eyes before meeting Alada's pleased appearance behind them.

"Perfect timing," Alada said with a noticeably calm tone in her voice.

Tierra nodded, still staring at the Nyas whose mouths had drooped open.

"I do not believe you all have met Gata de la Tierra, goddess of the Meus and the Bioluminescent Forest," Alada spoke.

One Nya stood and bowed, yet said nothing. Another then followed suit, and before long this cascaded into all the Nyas standing to bow their greetings.

Tierra stood still and merely nodded her head ever so slightly, though never breaking eye contact with the group itself.

"I was just explaining the dangers and circumstances at hand before your arrival. I am grateful for your impeccable timing," Alada continued, motioning for Tierra to enter the room fully and stand beside her.

Tierra surveyed the Nyas before her. "I sense they don't grasp the full weight of the situation," she stated, the fur prickling on the back of her neck.

"No, they do not," Alada said.

"And now?" Tierra asked, eyeing the council.

Alada remained silent, thus utilizing the quiet as an uncomfortable tool.

"And what would you have us do? Do you need an army? The Nyas are not one to hide or back down from a fight," the eldest Nya spoke.

Alada sat still. "I completely understand the Nya ways and means, sir."

He visible recoiled.

"I ask the Nya homeland to be on steady watch and guard outside … and inside. I also ask that the Nya's prepare the army for use or departure upon my notice should a circumstance arise where the need to defend the territories is deemed necessary," she continued.

"All raise your paw if you agree to the orders given by Goddess Alada," spoke one younger Nya.

Each within the council circle raised his or her paw.

"So be it," he spoke. "It will be done, your highness."

"Here is what else you must know," Alada continued, "The beasts have an ability to 'glitch' — as we call it," she looked to Tierra, "and this ability allows these beasts to teleport into any location and through barriers. This is why guards must be inside the sanctuary as well. There is no place they could not appear."

The council murmured amongst themselves.

"Is it only teleporting to and from?" one asked.

"No," Alada said. "It can also occur while fighting—like fighting a projection image or … a moving static image."

The murmuring continued.

"We have also experienced them staying slightly out of phase while fighting on one occasion," Tierra chimed in. "We couldn't land any hits and they then destroyed the community."

"I hardly expect much from the Meus of the forest in the ways of warriors," the eldest Nya retorted.

Without a thought, Tierra had let out a hiss loud enough to make the skin crawl on every being in the room. Her eyes, slit with rage, pierced the old, graying Nya before her.

"Any further degrading remarks from you, at any point, will result in your instant removal from the council on a permanent status," Alada spoke calmly, as if she were ordering tea and snacks.

Once again, he recoiled without so much as an apology.

"Tierra was also fighting, you old fool," the younger Nya stated.

Tierra glared at the elder, despite the conversation shifting elsewhere.

"Goddess Tierra," Alada began, "You must be in need of

food and drink after your journey. I will continue to provide details to the council and will soon join you and Birch for a hearty meal. Carnelian, please escort Birch and Tierra to the guest suites."

Tierra didn't remark or look at Alada as she walked out of the room with her shoulders back and her head high. She knew Alada had her back. Birch, also with his shoulders held high, strutted out of the room, not looking at the council members as he passed. As the doors closed behind them, they could hear discussions start up again. The party walked in silence as Carnelian led the way to the suites.

"There are three private bedrooms attached to a communal living room and a kitchen already stocked with necessary provisions," Carnelian commented upon arriving to the suite entrance. Tierra stepped over the threshold as Carnelian continued. "Goddess Tierra, you are most welcome in the land of the Nyas. I apologize for the rude welcome of some in the council, they do not always speak on behalf of all Nyas."

Tierra nodded, thanking him for the kind words. Carnelian then left, leaving them to rest and explore. Birch had taken a seat on a very comfy couch.

"Nice place. All white though," Birch said, then shivered. "Where's the central heating monitor — or at least a thousand blankets?" He began picking at the fabric of the overly-stuffed couch which had a snagged thread. "What do you think of the Nyas?" he asked, still picking the same spot. "Not exactly warm and welcoming like Alada." *Pick.*

Pick. Pick.

"I do not deny they are good warriors. Their assistance could be very useful in a tactical approach to this issue," Tierra said, filling a smaller, clean teacup with hot water from the sink.

Pick. Pick. Pick.

"So you don't like them," Birch remarked, now realizing he had made a small hole in the pristine white sofa. Something tiny and sharp poked out of the hole slightly, like that of the tip of a feather.

"I'm sure they're quite pleasant once you form a relation or connection," Tierra said, now adding some loose-leaf tea assortment into her cup, covering it with a small plate, intending it to simmer. She held the warm cup, impatient to drink it, when Birch let out a menacing hiss that filled the room.

Birch had continued to pick at the hole— until what was clearly a little feather stuck out just enough to get a claw grip on it. Birch's eyes slitted to an incomprehensibly thin degree. "These ... are ... the Northern ... Moss-Covered Sphynx bird ... FEATHERS!" His words were more hiss than audible voice. His breathing deepened and widened, and he contorted his face in a great effort to not explode. "This ... is an ... *endangered* species! Only found in the remote parts of the Northern Bioluminescent Forest..." His breathing was strangely loud. "I've been part of the endangered species committee, working to protect them for the last eight years!" he hissed and roared, "And now, I see

WHY — THEY — AREN'T — GROWING — in POP-ULATION!"

"Birch!" Tierra nearly dropped the cup onto the counter and began pleading for Birch to calm down, as he was now tearing open all the pillows and the couch itself to reclaim all the stolen feathers, screaming his full intention to return them to the Bioluminescent Forest for nesting materials.

"Birch! I hear you, okay?" Tierra pleaded, "I hear you." She didn't dare get in the middle of his tearing extravaganza. Feathers abound in the room, flying through the air, fluttering down to dust the entire room in white. "I didn't even know this was a species," she added, softly.

A roaring hiss emerged from Birch as he glared at her mid-tear of yet another cushion. "They claim we aren't good fighters," he hissed under his breath, "Yet they cowardly sneak into the Northern Bioluminescent Forest and steal and kill our birds that are incredibly important to our ecosystem!"

Tierra stood … unsure what to do, but a little impressed by his passion.

"I'll show them a fight. I'll start a *war*!"

She said nothing, realizing she couldn't reason with him now, trusting his tantrum would end … at some point. She again picked up her cup of warm tea, though some had spilled out, and began sipping while watching Birch's process.

Alada soon entered the room, surprised by the sight of the feathers absolutely everywhere, and seeing Birch stuffing the feathers into his pockets, his shirt, his pants, and waste baskets … and Tierra drinking tea calmly in the corner. Alada only managed to close the door behind her.

"How did you *not* know they were killing the Northern—" his words were garbled amongst his outpourings of feathers and struggles to bag them all up to go home.

She padded over and stood beside Tierra, who continued to sip her tea.

"What happened?" Alada whispered.

"He was cold," Tierra answered, sipping again. "And bored. He started picking at the cushion seams until he had ripped a hole."

Alada smiled and purred. "Well, yes, we don't have central heating, but there is a self-warming blanket in the ottoman … but what is with his madness?"

Hearing her, Birch quickly found and ripped the blanket up, thinking the feathers must be everywhere. "Are they in every mattress, couch, blanket, pillow, and room in this entire city?!" he roared.

Alada merely stood there, unsure what to think, while hoping no one would come in to see this. Tierra had finished her tea and placed the cup on a counter nearby, offering no explanation and acting as if nothing had happened. "How did the rest of the meeting go?"

The feathers started to settle, as did Birch's temper … sort of.

"Ah, well," Alada started, distracted, "Well enough. I have another tomorrow and then we can leave."

"But what about—" demanded Birch.

"These are all stuffed with the feathers of an endangered species. He has been on the committee for protecting them, so you can imagine … he's upset …" Tierra said.

Feathers continued to float and settle around the room.

"Yes…" Alada said, staring at Birch. "I will talk to the Nyas about this terrible occurrence, and I will ensure that no bird feathers are used that are on the endangered species list in any territory from here on out."

Satisfied, Birch stopped struggling to gather every single feather. As he calmed down, he sat back down on the shredded couch, sinking into the pile of feathers and began incessantly yawning. "Ahhh, this is quite warm for being in the mountains …. Alada, why weren't they very welcoming? When I was little, my parents always welcomed anyone into their h—" Birch plopped sideways on the couch mid-sentence and fell asleep, purring.

Tierra sat down next to the sleeping Birch, suddenly very interested in the coffee table's ornate wooden design. "Alsiprion?" she asked.

Alada nodded. "It's not endangered," she said, smiling as she proceeded to walk into her designated bedroom.

"You know," Tierra started, "not everything your Nyas have to say is completely wrong."

"I would expect not," Alada responded, having returned to the living room to retrieve pillows, which were now torn. "If this *is* so important, why don't we ask Coral and Ember for assistance? I know we'll be visiting them at some point, but would it not be better defending villages with the whole crew?"

Tierra paused. "You have a point."

"We should pick up Coral next, and leave Ember for last," she continued.

"Okay, we'll go."

Snnnore!!! Mmmf … erf.

Tierra moved over to make room for Alada, who took the hint and joined her on the tattered couch.

"Do you think the Nyas could handle the Phantom on their own?" Tierra asked.

Alada paused. "I don't know for sure, honestly. If you can't land a hit easily, even the best warriors may have little chance." Again, she paused for a moment. "My concern isn't with their capabilities. It is their being prone to arrogance that has me worried."

Tierra brushed some feathers off of Birch as she scooched closer, making more room for Alada. "How did they get so arrogant with you as their Guardian?"

"When arrogance isn't challenged, it can get out of hand. The truth is that they truly are very good at many things and have never met a force stronger than themselves in a very long time. I haven't challenged their arrogance because I recognized it primarily as deserved pride, but clearly that pride has grown into arrogance."

Tierra nodded.

"Like glitter," Tierra noted of the feathers she was still trying to brush off of Birch. "Like if glitter and static cling had a baby. What a mess."

Alada laughed harder than she should have. The joke wasn't that funny, but under duress, it was, in this moment, downright hilarious — a needed tension release.

Birch grumbled in his sleep, wiggling a bit as Tierra repeatedly smacked his body in attempt to remove feathers. She stopped trying to clean him off. "I think we're waking him. We should get to bed. Just let him sleep here."

Alada nodded, getting up. "Agreed." She stood, stretching. "Oh, did you need to eat? I'm surprised he fell asleep considering we had barely eaten all day."

"Tree traveling doesn't take much energy." Tierra also stood, yawning and stretching.

"Okay. Well, I'm going to find some fish and head to bed, then," Alada stated.

Tierra nodded. "Sounds good. Goodnight then." She sauntered off to the nearest bedroom and closed the door behind her.

"Goodnight."

Birch mumbled again.

"Goodnight, Birch." Alada said before turning toward the small kitchen to scavenge for food. "Feesh, feesh, feesh…" she mumbled to herself as she perused the refrigerated offerings. Behold, she found some fish — a prized bass, already seasoned. *No need to heat it up.* She ate it cold, which tasted divine. *Bed. Divine pillows. Sleep.* Visions of herself sleeping in a fluffy, comfy bed made her purr.

Chapter 23
Breakfast

Alada just couldn't stay asleep. She was home – actually inside the mountain after countless years – but … it didn't feel the same. Getting out of bed, she shuffled into the living room to find the couch empty. *Must have gone off to sleep in a proper bed,* she thought. Catching sight of the cavern outside the windows, she padded to the back door, and stepped outside, closing the door silently behind her.

The long hardwood balcony stretched out in either direction with railings adorned with tiny silver flowers. It wasn't morning yet, and the Nyas had found a way to project the outside atmosphere onto the ceiling of the cave itself. It looked like the nighttime sky with stars. There were so many—like someone had spilled a hundred jars full of glitter, creating the most beautiful masterpiece.

There are many pros and cons to being immortal, but it's the simplest things that bring the most awe … I've lived through countless seasons and have seen stars align…. Wouldn't it be wonderful if you could live in the sky? Dream in the stars and come down to the Earth when you wanted to…? There were so many things she could do, but for now, experiencing life's little offerings brought her the most contentment.

The sun had risen, and Alada woke up to the sound of a sizzling pan and a wafting, delectable smell.

Oh, jeez! I hadn't planned to fall asleep out here! Alada rushed inside and found Tierra and Birch making pancakes, fillet of rainbow tunafish, and eggs over easy.

"Morning," Tierra and Birch said together, as Birch grabbed the pan and started serving up everyone's plates.

Tierra then padded up to Alada and said in a quieter, teasing tone, "Fell asleep out there, did you?"

Alada stared down at the floor. "Yeah, I woke up from bed but accidentally fell back asleep out there." She looked around. "Wait, where did all the feathers go?"

"I tree traveled them back this morning before anyone woke up," Tierra answered. "Anyway, how was the sky projection? Last I remember, they were still working out all the glitches. It was just a black void with evenly spaced polka-dots last time."

"Just like the real thing," Alada said.

Birch smiled and opened the curtains to let in some light. "There's so much to explore! I mean—I wouldn't mind mimicking our homes in the forest like this, with proper regulation on feathers and respect for our fellow creatures. It's so well protected too! Is it weird for a Meu to like the mountains or is it just the underground system that's really fantastic?" he butted in.

"Well, I'm glad you're enjoying yourself, and I'm sorry to burst your bubble, but—" Alada cut in, seating herself into a chair by the dining table, "—but we're leaving later today."

"Good," he said, kicking a chair leg while sitting down next to Alada. "Ouch." Birch rubbed his foot, flattening his ears.

Tierra plopped next to the two of them and gobbled up all her food in a few moments. "Done! Gonna pack up my," she thought a moment about her belongings, which currently consisted of just her blender, "my … thing — now."

She left the room while Alada and Birch continued eating at a more leisurely pace.

And as if on cue, a loud scraping sound of metal against metal erupted from Tierra's room. "Ahhh! The auto-blending button I just installed! Eek, not my trophy! Why'd I store all my winnings in there?! Arg!"

Alada and Birch exchanged smiles, continuing to eat.

"Glad you slept well," said Alada.

Birch merely nodded a reply since he had just stuffed almost an entire fillet of fish in his mouth.

After finishing their quiet breakfast listening to Tierra's fun-filled activity list of what to do when they visit Coral at Lotus Bay, Birch brought over his and Alada's plate for cleaning, to which Tierra joined in to help clean the breakfast dishes.

Chapter 23

Knock, knock, knock!

Carnelian popped his head in.

"Pardon me, but is Goddess Alada the Great present?"

Tierra dropped a plate, and it clanged to the ground.

"Alada the Great? What do you need?" Tierra said, smirking.

Carnelian's eyes widened awkwardly as he stood in the doorway, not knowing if he should stay or just come back later.

This is another goddess, he thought. *Answer confidently.* "Well, her sacred shrine of holy Alada-ness is ready for her to give a speech — like she asked me to arrange last night."

Suddenly, Alada burst into the living area in her usual garb. "Off we go! Off we go!" Alada said peppily, then her eyes slid over to the smirking Tierra and confused Birch.

"I'd love to see this speech," Tierra smirked. "Can I come?"

"I'd love to *give* them a speech…" Birch murmured to himself.

Alada sighed. "Alright, you two can come along."

Chapter 24
The Refugees

When she made it to the side of the stage, having been stopped by a few questioning council members, she beheld Birch standing center stage pointing his paw at each Nya in turn. Tierra was already standing closer to him.

"… Just like you and me, they have friends and family they hope to return to every night. If you just go around mercilessly *murdering* these helpless birds to stuff your fancy couches, you're no better than the Phantom!" Birch spoke in a woefully shameful tone.

Tierra raised her paws, signaling for him to stop. "*Very* nice, Birch. Now, I'm sure everyone has been thoroughly informed of your endangered bird." Tierra caught sight of Alada and sighed with relief. "Oh, look, Goddess Alada's here!" She poked Birch. "Now please get off."

Birch took a quick sideways glance at Alada before climbing down from the stage, indicating that he was not quite satisfied with what he had accomplished. As he took his seat beside Tierra in the audience, the Nyas shuffled uneasily around him, murmuring to each other.

When Alada walked to the center stage, all the Nyas turned to her with a glowing anticipation — giving her confidence that they would get over Birch's … introduction … at some point.

She took a deep breath and began. "Hello, my dear Nyas! As you may or may not have heard from Birch, there is a threat known as the Phantom. Even though you all are very well-protected, thanks to our hard-working technicians, you still need to be vigilant and not blinded by pride."

Birch, instead of listening, had quietly started bickering with a female Nya, who he had assumed knew more about the Northern Moss-covered Sphinx bird than she was letting on.

"I know when I smell Bioluminescent-poppy candles; you can only get them where my friend lives—in the NORTH-ERN Bioluminescent Forest!" he hissed softly.

The other cat, who was just as infuriated as Birch, seemed just as passionate as him on the same subject.

"Well, well, well, Mr. Meu, this may be unbeknownst to *you*, but the Meus have been continuously fishing the endangered obsidian-scaled midnight salmon! Who migrate to the warmer waters of the Bioluminescent Forest for breeding season! We have been protecting their migration for a decade!" the female Nya hissed back. And in silent agreement, left the smaller venue to finish their debate somewhere else.

Within a few minutes, however, clapping rang out in the room, and Nyas began to file out surprisingly quickly.

"It's a good time to leave," Alada remarked, coming to stand beside Tierra. "We have more places to go." She looked around. "Where's Birch?"

Tierra shrugged. "He was arguing with a Nya over … other endangered species. Blame abounds." She walked off toward Birch's voice.

He was heavily discussing a new protective society as Tierra and Alada approached, who interrupted and stated the necessity to leave.

He hardly heard a word, but the Nya he was speaking with did. "You better go."

It barely occurred to him that she saw Alada and Tierra as goddesses, while he saw them as Holly and Jasmine … still. "Right," he said, "Okay. Let's go." He gave a shallow bow good-bye to the female Nya.

A small royal procession escorted them, including the council members, who lumbered along behind. Many blessings echoed as they marched off onto the far end path leading toward the coast. The forest soon swallowed them up from view.

"I've never met the goddess Coralees before," Birch began, kicking rocks like a kid in the back of the pack.

"She's very friendly," Alada stated. "You will like her."

"I sense you're going to see her as a goddess, unlike us," Tierra said laughingly, pointing to Alada and herself.

Birch didn't answer but bobbed his head around as he

thought. "You guys are more like … sisters. Or crazy cousins. Or undeveloped friends that are your sisters once removed. Or—"

"I'm going to stop you right there," Alada said, giving him a smile. "Yes, we are goddesses, but we are your friends. Let it be what it is."

He shrugged. "How many friends do you guys have?" he asked.

Alada and Tierra remained quiet.

"Define 'friend'," Tierra said slowly.

"You cannot be a goddess unless you love all," Alada spoke, remaining silent at the end.

"So just me, huh?" Birch said.

"Yup," Alada said, laughing. "And Tierra, Coralees …"

"I have JeffTree," Tierra laughed, thinking far back to the ugly tree friends she'd created. "It gets lonely and I'm a social butterfly. I always want to be around friends and fam—" She broke off and walked just a little slower, not looking at anyone.

No one spoke.

For a long time.

Birch continued kicking rocks as they walked, but he found himself repeatedly glancing toward Tierra, who continued to purposely not make eye contact with either of them.

"Were you guys always goddesses?" Birch asked, hesitantly. He wasn't sure how far was too far when it came to personal information.

Neither answered.

Apparently, that's far enough, he thought.

Once at the base of the mountain, they came across the healthy, raging Pearl River, known for the pearls releasing amongst the rapids from the rocks. Birch peered down into its icy depths.

"That Nya said you could find the Flaming Bass in this part of the Pearl River … hmm," he murmured. He paused in thought, then turned to Alada and Tierra. "We just follow this river to get to Lotus Bay, right? Maybe we can get a boat or something? Because, personally, I don't want to walk across a whole territory—and a desert at that. Bad things happen there, you know. I mean, Grandpa once told of a giant silver snake that hides in the Moto Desert waiting to eat you up! He said he saw it with his own two eyes, and some say it's the river itself!"

Tierra and Alada exchanged glances.

"I'm sure we'll be fine," Alada said simply.

"I miss Grandpa," Tierra said with a smile. "I wonder what crazy adventure that old Meu is on right now." She chuckled, clearly reminiscing about his stories.

"Alright … more walking.… What happened to those fancy Levi Lifts?" Birch said.

"They aren't on this side of the mountain. They mostly follow the edge of the Bioluminescent Forest when traveling to the bay. The sand makes it hard to tunnel," Alada responded.

"And why are we going this way?"

She didn't answer but *did* start walking along the river bank at a faster clip.

"Just because I'm your friend doesn't mean I'll walk everywhere, forever!"

No response.

"I *do* have limits…! You both know I'm a forest-kinda guy…"

No response.

"Walking! MY. ARCH. NEMESIS!"

Alada looked back at him. "Are you done yet?"

Birch paused, thinking, then said decidedly, "No, I'm not done. There are sooo many ways of traveling, and here we are. *Walking.*" He padded up from behind, which felt more ironic. "I feel like I'm slowing you down, now that I know you're goddesses." He kicked a few pebbles.

Tierra perked up. "Do you want to try tree traveling?"

Alada groaned loudly before clasping a paw over her mouth. "I mean, it's the best." She turned her head to hide a smile.

They stopped walking and faced one another.

Tierra's smile only got uncomfortably wider….

He viewed her large, toothy smile as a clear warning and said nothing for a moment as her smile did not fade, but her eyes widened slightly in anticipation. He felt afraid to say no, afraid to say yes … as he watched her eyes dilating.

"Traveling as the goddesses do … who else can say that?"

he said, bucking up his courage. "I can handle any type of travel you all do."

"I'll fly," Alada commented quickly.

Tierra grabbed his arm and led him to the nearest tree some meters away.

"Wait—" he tried to grab at Alada, "Why aren't you com—"

Alada was already off, exclaiming her destination and a cheer for them to have fun.

Birch didn't know how Tierra's smile could grow any wider as she positioned him in front of a tree. "You know, maybe I'll just—" But before he could finish, Tierra pulled him into the tree's bark and into a swirling void of leaves and light.

"Ahhhh!"

"Quit your yelling!" Tierra snapped, both of them briefly coming out of a tree, then immediately jumping into another. She pulled him tree through tree, traveling a great distance in a short amount of time.

"This. Is. The. *Wooooorst!*"

Tierra yanked on Birch's arm to silence him. "How many pieces do you want to cross this desert in? The options include: One, Two, or SEVEN! You are very distracting!" she said, her hair swooping in front of her face.

"Why did I let this happen?!" whined Birch.

"Okay, that's the last straw," Tierra hissed. She launched out of the palm tree with Birch flailing behind her, then flung him — unceremoniously — off like that sack of awkward guilt-feathers she'd returned to the Bioluminescent Forest that morning.

He landed with a loud splash in a shallow lake.

Tierra landed beside him, brushing bark off her arms and surveying the dry terrain. "Welcome to the Moto Desert," she muttered. "Hydration not included… unless you count that." She nodded at the lake.

When Birch's head resurfaced, his face was shining with glee. "Ah. You know, that whole thing was quite — refreshing! Now I smell like a lovely mix of freshly cut pine and … birch! We really should do that more often; it doesn't leave a mark!" He purred while getting out of the water. "I haven't been this clean in weeks! This really *does* beat walking."

"So, does that mean you'll stop yelling?" Tierra said hopefully.

"Maybe. Do you think yelling makes it more exciting?"

Tierra didn't respond, but *did* smile.

Birch shook out his fur. "Where are we? Lotus Bay?"

Tierra, however, didn't answer, she was looking fixedly in one direction — unblinking, with her pupils slitted. He found himself looking from her to the direction of her stare.

Before them both, beyond the sacred pools of Ember's private sanctuary, were freely roaming beasts, and the more they looked — the more beasts they saw. Before long, they realized the beasts numbered more than they could keep track of as they kept coming and going, and moving, and changing directions as they meandered the once mellow pathways of the Oasis.

"When did these get here!?" Birch asked in a forced whisper.

No answer.

"Where are all the Aras?"

No answer.

"How come Ember's letting them wander like this?"

No answer.

"What's going on? Why—"

Tierra pulled him into the tree without a word, and he didn't thrash or groan or complain until she pulled him out of the last tree some twenty feet from a now resting Alada.

"You're a little late," Alada calmly spoke, though she quickly looked around Tierra to see how Birch had handled such a trip. "Enjoy tree traveling?"

Birch bounded forward, showcasing his clean and vibrant fur, temporarily forgetting all about the beasts. "Yes!" he exclaimed, "I smell so nice! Look at this sheen on my coat. That is definitely my favorite way to travel." He admired his own fur. "You should try it sometime. It may be even faster than flying!"

Alada merely half-smiled as she recalled her own experience with tree traveling. Oh, the stickiness.

"Turns out it's vastly less sticky for native Meus," Tierra mentioned, standing before her. "Now, did you see the—"

Voices in the not-so-distant distance emerged as a band of Aras appeared on the path with lovely sand-colored furs, whitish spots and cream-colored robes.

"What are they doing here on the outskirts of Lotus Bay?" Alada asked.

"I know. We need to talk more about this," said Tierra.

"But is this a coincidence or what?"

"We'll talk."

Alada joined Tierra and Birch in standing as the Aras skeptically approached.

"Greetings," Alada said, holding up her hands in a traditional Ara greeting of peace.

They timidly replied to the greeting as they drew nearer, but they kept their distance.

"We're not goddesses," Tierra whispered to Birch. "Keep that in mind. It feels important to treat us as Holly and Jasmine while we're with them."

"Why?"

"Just a feeling it's important. *Please.*"

He slightly nodded while keeping his eyes locked on the Aras — for he had never met an Ara before.

"We are traveling to the nearest coast," an Ara spoke. "Do you know how much farther?"

Alada took point and easily conveyed the short distance and direction. "We are headed there as well, if you would appreciate some company?"

The Aras did not appear to appreciate the idea of additional company, as they stood rigid, unanswering.

"I must say, it is a rare treat to meet a group of Aras, as your clans rarely leave the Oasis," Alada spoke.

And this is a rare opportunity to gather intel on the beasts, Tierra thought.

Again, the Aras appeared visibly untrusting and quite

scrutinous of their appearance. "We are escaping the enslavement and takeover of the Oasis by Umbrakin."

Alada couldn't hide her shock, but Tierra stepped forward and whispered to her, "It's true. I was just about to tell you how we stopped in the Oasis — cause of *someone's* complaining — and we saw them. Hundreds. I can confirm their statement."

I see what she was trying to say earlier, Alada thought, trying to remain composed.

"But what *are* they—the Umbrakin?" Alada whispered.

"I think that's what the beasts call themselves," Tierra remarked.

"I'm more concerned about the enslavement—we have had no form of slavery for more than a thousand years." Alada's eyes narrowed as she glanced back in the direction of the Oasis.

"Well, it seems to have come back again," the Ara said stiffly. "The Umbrakin have completely taken over the Oasis and the villages everywhere else here."

"When did they get here, and how?" Tierra asked, her brow furrowing.

An Ara guard stepped forth. "They started arriving in large groups, one group at a time over a few days. I have no idea where they came from. No one does. They just appeared. We tried to fight them off." He glanced somberly around his group. "Clearly, it didn't work. We lost a great many from our Guard. We prayed for help, but Ember had left us before their arrival, and we haven't seen him since," he ended bitterly.

"Since the last full moon," another Ara added.

Three weeks, Alada thought.

Alada and Tierra made eye contact for a brief moment. It wasn't unusual for Ember to disappear, but why at a time like this? He had never left them defenseless, despite his issues.

"I'm glad you escaped to claim your freedom," Tierra said after a few moments of silence. "The coast is a good place to go to."

"We want to be as far away from anyone else—" an Ara began before being interrupted by an unruly, younger kitten.

"And far, far away from any of the gods," the kitten said with a bitter hiss.

"Well, if you're going to the ocean to get away from everyone," Tierra said, "You should be aware there's a large population of Mizus there."

The Aras looked at each other — clearly trying to decide between water and privacy.

"You've all been through a lot, clearly," Alada said gently. "There is a lot of protection in that area. We can recommend a path that will lead you up onto the cliff sides that overlook the ocean. They may have the privacy and protection you are looking for. However, it is best that the Mizus are told of your presence."

The Aras agreed to making their presence known to the leaders of the Mizus and furthermore agreed to walking together toward Lotus Bay.

The overly vocal kitten continued to rant about the incompetence of their god and the goddesses as they walked.

Everyone heard her.

The whole time.

Tierra couldn't help but smirk here and there at the overly repugnant comments of such a young kitten with no real-world experience. Her parents did not ask her to tone down her apparent bias but instead condoned it with examples of their experiences with how terribly mistreated they were by Guardian Ember — refusing to refer to him as any type of god — while emphasizing their distrust of the other goddesses when no help came during said mistreatment.

Tierra nor Alada truly found these comments to be hurtful, but they could tell Birch felt extremely uncomfortable as he continuously interjected overly magnanimous portrayals of the goddesses' generosity of spirit and kindness.

"The goddesses are extremely caring and generous," Birch commented after a particularly nasty comment of their supposedly selfish nature from the tiny kitten. "They truly want the best for all their realms, and even though *some* cats and kittens don't always see what's right in front of them, it doesn't mean that the goddesses are ignoring them completely. Maybe they are listening but aren't allowed or can't interfere. Maybe they choose to stay quiet because they know that the cats *around* them cannot understand what they have to say in the moment … but they are the most caring, although sometimes a little too competitive—" he glanced at Tierra, "They do their best, and are learning and growing, just like all of us."

"Thank you for the soliloquy of admiration, Birch," Alada commented, still wondering exactly what had happened to Ember, and why he wasn't trying to do something about the invading beasts.

"I'm sure the goddesses appreciate your sentiment and hear you clearly, as they choose to listen to everyone's perspectives," Tierra stated with a delicate smirk.

"That's just the problem," the mother of the kitten spoke, "The goddesses and Guardian Ember — they're not above selfishness. They, too, can fish for whatever makes the ego smile — even at the expense of their own people."

Tierra shrank a little — remembering back to Tierra Town and the dancing she did instead of warning them of the impending danger. Flashes of the attack came into mind and her smile faded. Alada noticed how Tierra's stature shrank under the weight of the mother's comment.

"Indeed! That sort of thing may happen," Birch loudly proclaimed, "But we must understand that they, too, have their own burdens to carry as they have chosen to care for us all. What an enormous responsibility they carry upon their delicate shoulders, except Ember, who has clearly decided to…" he trailed off. "Not all the gods make good choices, but as their kindred spirits, we must also help ourselves in times of great peril."

The party said nothing, to which Birch took as a sign of agreement and continued. Though no one was really listening, Alada appreciated his clear dedication to not offending herself or Tierra. However, as Birch continued, the little kitten argued back more and more, which was encouraged by the kitten's mother with nods and uh-huhs of agreement.

"He only sends out orders, laws and more rules via half-burnt parchment notices," another Ara spoke. "We were banned from the ponds and only allowed water from the trickling river, which is also drying up."

"Birch—stop bickering with a kitten," Tierra finally spat, interrupting the adult Ara to address the momentarily childish Birch, whose in-favor goddess opinions were riling the kitten.

Alada took him aside and let the party pass. "They've been through enough," she whispered. "It's okay to let them process their feelings of betrayal." They continued to walk in the far back of the group.

"But these are lies, not processing," Birch retorted.

Alada shrugged. "Perhaps these feelings will change soon enough. Showing our real identity in this moment will not fix their feelings, but may likely enrage them because we're here *after* they saved themselves. We weren't there when they truly felt they needed us."

"But you didn't know."

Alada shrugged once more. "It doesn't matter that we didn't know."

Birch fell silent, thinking. "Why didn't you know? Isn't there a… like… a prayer network?" He had used his hands to try to explain it, but ended up just waving them around as if confused.

"Not really," she said. "Though I feel we should have felt something because we have in the past. I don't know what happened. The truth is that we don't always know. I don't know why Tierra didn't get the message that Stone Creek was under massive attack. I'm sure someone tried to get her attention." She, too, walked quietly, thinking.

They hadn't noticed that Tierra had also allowed herself to join them in the back.

"I don't know, either," Tierra remarked, tears in her eyes. "But I am truly sorry." She stared at Birch, who stared at her. They had somehow stopped walking and stood, staring.

"We are Guardians, not goddesses. Goddesses is just a term that was picked up along the way because of our abilities, but those are the abilities of the Guardians. This is why we have flaws. This is why we need to eat. This is why we aren't perfect," Alada said quietly.

Birch still stared at Tierra and he heaved a trembling breath. "I forgive you."

Chapter 25

Lotus Bay

Alada overheard a few of the Aras quietly reminiscing about their escape — and the mysterious absence of their Guardian, Ember.

They all walked until dusk and set up a simple camp.

"We'll get to the split in the trail by mid-morning," Alada commented, passing out food after camp had been set. "Probably only a couple of hours' walk left to that point."

The air now carried with it the salt of the sea and a natural refreshment to the spirit.

"I look forward to seeing this place," Birch commented. "I haven't been to Lotus Bay before."

The Aras were mostly silent, keeping to themselves the caretaking of one another, which Alada witnessed with pleasure.

"You have a beautiful family," Alada soon commented to the mother.

"There are three families here," the mother remarked, nodding her head in appreciation. "And a few of Ember's old guard, who agreed to accompany us to safety. Many of the guards are leaving one or two at a time with escaping families."

"Very noble."

The mother nodded as her kitten approached. "Mommy, watch this!" she said as she tossed her body into a half-cartwheel. "Ta-da!" she purred.

Alada clapped quietly at the little Ara's success. "She's quite the acrobat."

"Indeed, she is. Her and her friend used to build miniature obstacle courses for each other, well, before those awful beasts took them down, taking over the space for more of their sleeping tents."

The little kitten curled in her mother's lap and fell asleep almost instantly. The soft conversation dimmed into silence as those within the party fell asleep under the stars. Only Alada remained awake — alone in the darkness of the snuffed-out fire. She sat quietly, listening to the muffled snores and deep breathing of the others. After she ensured everyone was asleep, she leaned over to Tierra and woke her with a gentle nudge.

"Aladaaa, I was sleeping…"

"Let's discuss. We need to talk."

"Whas goin' on?" she yawned, straightening up a bit.

"We need to try and find Ember, and find out what he's up to."

Tierra sighed drowsily. "You know, I just thought of something. What if he is trying to find the Phantom and just made the stupid decision to leave the Aras unprotected?"

Alada pondered the possibility. "You're right. That would make sense. Although, I would still like to know where he is at least. He should have notified us of the beasts arrival and his leaving."

"Coralees may have an idea. She has all sorts of techy whatnot. Maybe she has some sort of EmberTracker5000 we aren't aware of."

"You're right, we'll be able to figure more out with her help."

"I wonder if she has something like a BeastBasher or a PhantomFwaper …"

"Tierra?" Alada said in a we-need-to-get-back-to-the-topic voice.

"Sorry."

"Anyway, we probably need to get to bed. Rest is important."

"Says the person who woke me up."

"Well, we needed to talk sometime by ourselves, but I'm sorry none the less."

"Thank you. Best be off to sleep. Good night!" With that, Tierra flopped back down on her soft — feather free — pillow, and fell right back to sleep, snoring faintly.

Alada smiled. "Good night to you, too." Her gentle blue gaze swept over the group of peacefully slumbering cats, pausing longer on Birch, Tierra, and the Ara guard who was trying to keep watch on the outskirts of camp. She watched as he fiercely fought back the sleep he needed. She made a mental note to wake up in a few hours and continue guarding; she was a Guardian after all. Once again, she smiled before lying down to drift off to sleep under the stars.

By morning, the Aras were not only awake, but had silently readied themselves — waiting, in fact — for the others to wake and rise.

"Morning, I see you're all … ready," Birch commented, sitting up and rubbing the sleep from his eyes.

The Aras sat silently on a nearby log before answering. "It is our nature to rise before the sun and do the bulk of the day's work before the heat," the Ara guard stated.

Birch, Alada, and Tierra all readied themselves without eating breakfast, joining the Aras to set off as quickly as possible.

Tierra posted herself with the Ara guard near the front, while Alada amused herself more with the kitten's antics, and Birch wandered in the back observing the change in fauna, funga, and flora he hadn't noticed before.

Within a few hours, as Alada had predicted, a fork in the road appeared ahead.

"I think this is where we will part ways," said Tierra. "We have someone we need to meet, and that other path will take you to the ocean cliffs."

The leader of the party nodded. "We thank you for accompanying and leading up us up to this point. But indeed, let us say our goodbyes. Time for us to go our separate ways." The Ara shook Tierra's paw, and then led the rest of the Aras off on the left path. Alada and Birch raised their paws, waving as they left.

"May you all find comfort and peace in your new home!" Alada called.

Now alone, Alada, Birch, and Tierra started down the shaded path on the slope to the right.

The salt-sap trees grew denser here, and finally they could spot the ocean through the narrow strips of light between the tree trunks. The dusty dirt path they trod on soon gave way to a solid walkway of cobblestone and the surrounding ground grew lush with grasses and different bushes. After a while more of walking in silence, they came upon a wooden sign which read: Dragon Fish Cove: quarter mile.

Birch studied the sign. "Dragon Fish Cove? Did we already cross the border?"

"Yes, we've been in Lotus Bay for a while now. Now come on, Birch, we're almost there," Alada said, walking on ahead.

After a quarter mile, the entrance to the town of Dragon Fish Cove soon came into view with its large arch made of multi-colored metal, glass, and polished stones. Inside were little rounded shops and houses with lightly colored paint, and each of them had a stained-glass window with intricate designs etched neatly within them. The sides of most of the buildings had colorful murals of sea life, forests, mushrooms, and depictions of their goddess Coralees. The sky above was a crisp shade of blue with a few broken clouds here and there, and carried on the gentle breeze was the refreshing aroma of the salty ocean water. It was a peaceful town—a little *too* peaceful.

No one was there.

Birch poked his head into a bakery. "Hello?" He sniffed, smelling … nothing. "Why's nobody here?" he called out to Alada.

Tierra and Alada came close.

"Don't ask me," Tierra said, shrugging.

Then, a voice rang out behind them — clear, amused, and unfamiliar.

"Yes, don't ask her. Ask me."

About the Author

Elora Sofia

Award-winning thirteen-year-old author and illustrator best known for:

 **Literary Titan Book Awards**

 **2024 Scholastic Art & Writing**

A passionate storyteller since early childhood, Elora has been drawing, storyboarding, and building rich worlds through her art and writing for as long as she can remember.

Elora has spoken at multiple schools and appeared on several media podcasts to share her journey as a young author. She is currently studying storyboarding under a professional storyboard artist and graphic design with a commercial designer.

Elora is available for public speaking engagements and commissioned illustration work, including children's books, middle grade fiction, graphic novels, and comic books.

www.elorasofia.com

GUARDIANS OF FELINA

The Lost Lair

A New Adventure Awaits!

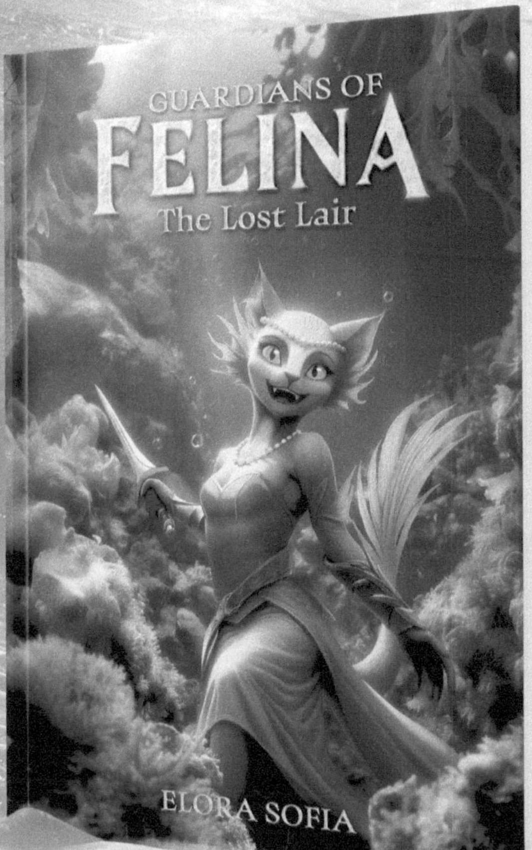

GUARDIANS OF
FELINA
The Lost Lair
ELORA SOFIA